Right
Click

SUSAN AYLWORTH

Right Click

a novel

Covenant Communications, Inc.

Cover image *Geek Chic* © Chih Hang. Courtesy of istockphoto.com

Cover design copyrighted 2009 by Covenant Communications, Inc.

Published by Covenant Communications, Inc.
American Fork, Utah

Printed in Canada
First Printing: September 2009

16 15 14 13 12 11 10 09   10 9 8 7 6 5 4 3 2 1

ISBN 10: 1-59811-731-9
ISBN 13: 978-1-59811-731-8

For Becca and Jonathan, Paul and Carly, John and Amy, and always, for Roger.

Acknowledgments

Special thanks to Anonna Hubbard, Patricia Kimsey, Rebecca and Jonathan Wright, Matt and Marie Aylworth, and Sue Lucas—family, friends, and superb story consultants. And always to my husband, Roger, who understands. Thank you all.

Chapter 1

"So we agree then," my sister Ruth was saying. She lifted her red plastic tumbler full of cherry Kool-Aid. "Let's toast to it."

We were standing in the kitchen of my little house in South Jordan, where we had just finished covering the dreary walls in a sunny buttercup yellow. Apparently we had also just finished sorting through my dreary love life.

"A toast," Ruth repeated, waving her Kool-Aid like a talisman. Though neither of us has ever had a sip of alcohol in our lives, Ruth is always toasting to one thing or another. I think it makes her feel sophisticated. "Come on," she prompted.

I lifted my bright blue tumbler. "Uh, what exactly did we agree to?" I had the sense I'd skipped a couple of crucial scenes.

"We agreed," Ruth said with that oh-how-you-weary-me tone in her voice, "that you are going to climb out of the rut you've been in for the last half year and get back on the horse that threw you."

I hesitated. "Is that a mixed metaphor?"

Ruth blew out a weary sigh. "Metaphor, schmetaphor. The point is, you've been in a funk ever since what's-his-name—"

"Kyle," I reminded. "Rhymes with guile."

"Or lack of style," Ruth added. When it came to Kyle Lewis, we had no trouble coming up with rhymes—as long as they were ugly. "Anyway, you're going to forget the creep and start dating again." She cocked an eyebrow. "The problem isn't going to go away just because you ignore it."

I bit back a retort about the wisdom of taking romantic advice from one's eighteen-year-old sister. In the most general sense, Ruth was right. I'd wasted more than enough energy on the fiancé from outer darkness. It was time to find more joy in my life. I pasted on a smile. "You're right," I said, ceremoniously tapping my plastic tumbler to hers. "It's time to get back out there. The trick is in figuring out how."

She grinned and gulped a quick swallow. "Oh, that's no problem. I have the answer right here." She started rummaging in her purse, the kind designed to carry your standard year's supply.

I managed to swallow my groan. "Don't tell me you have a man in there?"

"Cute, Sarah. Real cute." She continued rooting through things and emerged a half minute later with a clipping torn from a newspaper. "Voilà!" she announced and dangled it before my eyes.

"Find your eternal companion," I read aloud. "We have someone for everyone." My curiosity piqued, I skimmed through the rest of the ad, my skepticism growing with each line. "You've gotta be kidding. A computer dating service?"

"Not just any service. It's Mormons2Marry.com. They'd only set you up with the kind of guys you'd want to marry—you know, returned missionaries, priesthood holders—"

"Need I remind you that Kyle was both of those?" I heard the acid in my voice and felt a little guilty for turning it on my sister, but a reality check seemed in order.

"Point taken. However, I think you have to trust that jerks like Beelzebub Lewis are one-to-a-customer, and you've already had yours."

"Really, thanks for thinking of me, but I'll have to get a lot more desperate before I let a computer set me up. Besides, how good can these people be? They've even got the 'm-word' in their title. No self-respecting LDS single is going to go for that."

"People *are* going for it, lots of them," Ruth defended, her eyes narrowing. "If you don't do this, how are you going to meet somebody?"

"Need I remind you that we're living in Latter-day central? I could meet Mr. Right just walking down the street tomorrow or standing in line in the grocery store, or—"

"It hasn't worked so far."

I set down my Kool-Aid, trying to suppress the image of a knife poking out of my chest. "You've got me there."

"Some of the girls on my floor have older brothers," Ruth offered. I had a momentary vision of a date arranged by a couple of teenaged matchmakers from Helaman Halls. It wasn't pretty.

"Uh, thanks anyway."

"But Sarah—"

"Look, honey. You've made your point. I need to get back into circulation, but I need to do it on my own timetable."

"I thought you wanted to get married in this lifetime," Ruth retorted, her voice sullen. She started picking up paintbrushes.

"You've got a mean streak, you know that?" I said as I followed her lead.

* * *

I was just leaving for school the next morning when the phone rang. It was our older sister, Deb. "I hear you're going to start dating again," she said as soon as I picked up. There are no secrets in my family.

"Sounds like Ruth has been talking."

"Ruth? I heard it from Wendy. She got it from Denise." She was referring to two of our sisters-in-law, married to my brothers Tim and Seth.

"Tell me this: Is there anyone on the Wasatch Front who hasn't heard it yet?"

"I don't know about the whole front," Deb said, ignoring my sarcasm, "but I think the Salt Lake Valley is pretty well saturated."

"Great! Why don't I just buy a billboard?" I glanced at my watch, glad I'd gotten an early start.

"Not a bad idea," Deb answered, "but they're kind of expensive. There are a few other things we can try before we reach that point."

"Really, Deb . . . Hey, wait a minute!" I replied. "Where does the *we* come in? This is *my* future we're talking about."

"Which is why we need to get started right away," she answered ever so reasonably. "You know what they say about Mormon men beyond a certain age . . ."

"I hesitate to ask."

"They're like parking spaces," Deb answered. "The good ones are taken, and the rest are either too far out there or emotionally handicapped."

I chuckled despite myself. "Okay, I'll agree with you on that one, but I'm not even twenty-four yet. It's not like I'm over the hill or anything."

"You want the statistics? I heard them on the radio the other day. The median age for a woman's first marriage is 22.8—"

I groaned. "Spare me the details. Look, I've got to get to school. You don't want twenty-two third graders running around unsupervised. Besides, I'm still new there. I have to make a good impression."

"Good point," Deb answered. "I'll go to work on this and get back to you later, okay?"

"Not really," I answered, knowing it wouldn't make a bit of difference.

* * *

"Miss Kimball? Can I get another book from the library?" I looked up to find Ellen Brenner at my desk.

"Don't tell me you've already finished *Black Beauty?*" I asked. The girl was ripping through our beleaguered school library like Sherman through Georgia. At this rate, she'd run out of new material before Halloween.

"Last night," Ellen answered, showing me the book.

"Let's see," I said, trying to recall details. "You've already read all the Marguerite Henry books, right?"

"Yeah, and most of Walter Farley. I didn't finish *The Island Stallion Returns* because of—well, you know."

"Um, yes," I answered. Ellen had missed out on the last half of the tale about the exquisite red stallion on a desert island after her twin, Lillian, dropped the book in the toilet. "Have you tried Jack London? I think you'd enjoy *Call of the Wild.*"

"Is it about a horse?"

"A dog," I answered, "but it's a great story."

"I might try that," Ellen answered. "I like dogs, too. So can I go to the library?"

I resisted the urge to correct her with "*may* I go," something I'd always resented my teachers for doing. "Sure," I said, "but it's almost lunchtime. Can you wait another ten minutes? Then you may go to the library after you eat." I felt smug, having modeled the correct phrase, just as I'd been taught in my teacher prep program. Not that I'm always the model of perfect grammar, mind you. I just like to pat myself on the back when I get it right.

"Great," Ellen said, her expression brightening. She scurried back to her desk and began organizing it, meticulously arranging each item.

Most of the other kids in my class were still finishing their arithmetic papers, but Ellen had whipped through hers in minutes, checked the answers against the key I keep at my desk (another perfect paper), then polished off her spelling homework. She reminded me of me when I was her age, and it wasn't just the tendency toward academic overachievement, either. There was also the matter of her twin.

As if conjured by my thoughts, Lillian Brenner appeared. "Miss Kimball?"

"Yes, Lillian?"

She held up her worksheet, only about three-quarters finished. "I just don't get number fourteen. How do you do that again?"

I stifled a sigh and began explaining once more how to carry numbers. It was probably the sixth time I'd been through it that morning. As Lillian returned to her desk, her brow as furrowed as a poorly plowed field, I pondered the vagaries of the genetic grab bag. Would-be parents dipped into the gene pool, never knowing what they'd pull out. Two perfect examples were Ellen and Lillian, twins as different in appearance as in academic gifts.

While Ellen was shorter than the average third grader, prone toward chubbiness, and had baby-fine brownish hair that always seemed to need a comb, Lillian was blessed with a tall, willowy frame, perfect hair, and enviable Scandinavian blondeness. Though the boys in the class still made a fuss about girls and cooties, every one of them made excuses to be close to Lillian, sometimes even fetching and carrying things for her when they thought the other guys weren't watching. On the playground or in the lunchroom, she was always the center of attention. Even the sixth graders noticed her—a problem, since few of them feared cooties anymore. Ellen, on the other hand, was going to need all the smarts she'd been blessed with. Not that she was unattractive. She was pretty enough in her own quiet way, but with Lillian around, no one noticed.

I knew just how she felt, though my sisters were never the problem. Deb, gorgeous from birth, was eight years older and had never been a threat, having been married and out of the house by the time I was twelve. Even Baby Ruth, beauty queen that she was—a finalist for Miss Utah—was enough younger than me to avoid being direct competition. It was my best friend, Jeanie, who had always cast me—albeit unintentionally—in the Ugly Duckling role. In the beginning, I'd wondered why Kyle had wanted me instead of her. In the past half year, I'd come to wish he hadn't—then felt horrible for wishing him on Jeanie. Since he'd left me to marry "the girl from home," I'd watched girls like Ellen, wondering whether some of us were born to be alone.

The lunch bell rang, derailing my dismal train of thought, and I stood, hoping to calm the scramble for the lunch line while it was still in its formative stages. I lifted my hand above my head, crossing my fingers in the agreed-upon signal for attention. "Settle down, everyone. You know we can't leave until your desks are orderly and you've taken your proper places."

The announcement had its hoped-for effect, and the roar eased into a quiet hum, the scramble into an orderly line. "That's better," I pronounced, remembering to reward the positive. "Any of you who haven't finished and checked your worksheets can complete them during independent work time this afternoon." I looked out at twenty-two expectant, upturned faces. "Good work, class. Henry, you were exceptionally good this morning. You may lead the line to the lunchroom."

Beaming, Henry Jackson stepped into the lead, and I opened the door, the Ugly Duckling all grown up, now Mother Duck following her brood toward the feeding pens and wondering whether I'd spend the rest of my life raising other people's children.

* * *

On fast Sunday, we always had a gathering of the Kimball clan, all the children and grandchildren coming back to Mom and Dad's to break our fast with a potluck dinner. Deborah and Brian drove down the ridge from Sandy, while Josh and Barbara drove up from Provo, now with Ruth in tow. It was a custom set in stone, and the only member of our family who had an adequate excuse for not showing up was my brother Mark, who was presently assigned to the Texas San Antonio Mission.

So it was that on this last Sabbath of September (an early fast Sunday due to general conference the next week), seven of the eight of us gathered at the family home in Draper, together with Mom and Dad, the four in-laws, and all thirteen of the next generation. I'd spent longer than I expected studying my Relief Society lesson for the next week and left later than I had planned, and so, because of unexpected traffic on 106th South, my fruit salad and I were among the last to arrive. I discovered as soon as I entered that the folks who were gathered before me had not been wasting time.

"Hello, darling," Mom said as she answered the door. "Look, everyone! Sarah's here!" Then she turned back to me. "I hear you're dating again."

Mom had always taught us it was rude to roll our eyes, so I had to look away as I answered, "Well, not yet . . ."

"Sarah!" My brother Josh stepped forward and took the salad out of my hands. "I thought we'd starve waiting for you. So have you got any good prospects in the dating department?"

"Uh, not yet," I said again. By the time I made it to the dining room, I was blushing furiously, I'd said "not yet" at least six more times, and I had already heard about three different "eligible men" I really had to meet. I glowered at Ruth as we took our places at the table, but she either pretended not to see me or her perceptiveness meter was turned down low. Either way, she went right on regaling the family with the story of how she had helped me paint my kitchen and had changed my life in the process, ending with the comment, "Now we won't have to hear Sarah complain about Kyle anymore."

I felt myself swelling up like a puff adder and was just about to respond when Dad asked my brother Noah to say the blessing. Noah, who was sitting beside me at the table, took my hand while he said the prayer, reminding me that it could be a good thing to have family. When he finished to a chorus of "Amen," Ruth jumped right back in. "So anyway, we're finally getting Sarah out of her depression. Now if I can just get her to sign up for the dating service I found—"

"Really, Ruthie. No one wants to hear about Mormons2Marry.com," I said, not sure what I wanted more—the opportunity to fade into the woodwork or the chance to throttle Ruth.

"I do," Noah said.

I turned to him with a gasp. "Noah! Don't encourage her."

"I think it's a good idea," he defended. "I'm signing up."

I stared at him, then realized my mouth was hanging open and purposefully lifted my jaw. "You're kidding, right?" I looked around the table at the faces of my loved ones, all waiting for Noah's reply.

"Not at all," he said, not even seeming to realize he had just entered the ranks of famous traitors, right up there next to Benedict Arnold.

"Noah . . ." I couldn't even think of anything to say.

"I think it's a great idea." It was Denise, Seth's wife. "It's a way to narrow down the prospects—you know, make the whole process easier."

"That's one of the things computers do well," Wendy, Tim's wife, agreed. I couldn't believe they were all acting like Ruth's dating service was a sane, reasonable idea.

"It's ridiculous!" Everybody turned, responding to my outburst. "I mean, Noah's a great guy—returned missionary, college graduate, handsome, ambitious, hard-working in a great job. He's buying his own home and—"

"You don't have to sell us," Deb said. "We all love Noah."

I turned to my brother. "Noah, the last thing you need is a computer to help you find women. An attractive guy like you—"

"Sarah," he said, laying his hand on my arm. "It isn't about finding women; it's about finding the *right* women. I mean, you get to be a certain age, and—"

"I don't want to hear the parking spaces joke," I said, wondering if someone had been handing out crazy pills. "Noah, you're only twenty-five!"

"Sarah, would you pass around the casserole, please?" It was Mom, effectively changing the subject. "Tim, make sure the children get the fruit salad, will you?"

"Sure, Mom," Tim said, taking my salad to the children's table. The conversation turned to everyone's plans for general conference, Ruth's change of major from child development to sociology, and everyone else's plans for the upcoming month. I listened with half an ear but kept casting furtive glances at Noah, wondering if he could possibly be serious. Was I the only person in America who still believed love couldn't be mechanized? Just as that thought hit me, a second one followed, and I realized to my chagrin that a machine probably couldn't do much worse for me than I'd done for myself. I resolved to put Baby Ruth's dating service on the back burner but to at least keep it in mind. Maybe, if I got desperate enough . . . I shuddered as I passed the green beans.

By Sunday evening, I had more or less come to terms with my status as the new family project. I had also decided there was no reason to make more of the dating matter than necessary. After all, I'd been right in what I'd said to Ruth about living in Mormon central. If I just paid attention to the interesting men around me, maybe asserted myself a little . . .

* * *

By the time I sat down to watch the first conference session the following Saturday, I had smiled prettily at three different married men (who just happened to not be wearing wedding rings), suggested dinner to our local letter carrier (only to find out he was engaged), and asked the handsome fourth grade teacher down the hall if he'd like to take in a movie sometime (only to have him show me a photo of his partner, Ralph). Ruth's dating service was looking better all the time.

I was still feeling embarrassed and highly unlovable as I sat down to watch conference, but by the time the choir had sung the opening song, the peace of the gospel was already settling in around me. Sometimes I wondered how nonbelievers got through even the simplest of life's problems. Over the course of the weekend, I soaked up every session, grateful that for at least a little while I was able to see my situation in the context of eternity, where it didn't seem so bad after all.

One other thing happened during conference—one I wasn't ready for. Two different speakers dealt with the doctrine of forgiveness and our need to pardon all who trespass against us. As I sat listening to the second talk, the Spirit whispered that I still had some work to do. At first, I was startled; I mean, I like to think of myself as a fairly forgiving person. Then I was struck by a memory, an image of Kyle as I'd last seen him, and I felt the bile rise in my throat.

"Okay," I answered aloud. "You're right. I still have some work to do." But even as I said the words, I knew I still needed time. I just didn't feel ready to come to terms with Kyle's betrayal—not yet. That evening I wrote it all in my journal: how I'd been impressed by the conference talks and the more personal lessons I'd been taught, and how someday soon I would have to deal with the anger I still felt. It embarrasses me now, but I also wrote, "Kyle doesn't deserve my forgiveness after what he did."

Monday morning came, and I put on a new attitude with my first autumn sweater, preparing myself to face the coming week with a smile but without the need to "find someone." If it happened, it happened. If not, well, it would happen in the Lord's good time. Resolved to enjoy my week, I focused on the task of teaching Lillian Brenner how to multiply and quickly realized that could keep me plenty busy all by itself.

Chapter 2

I should have smelled a setup even before I smelled Seth's famous barbeque sauce, but Seth and Denise had invited me to weeknight dinners before, so I remained blissfully clueless until their doorbell rang a few moments after I arrived. I was still in the entryway taking off my coat when Seth, eyes twinkling, answered the door, then introduced Ron, a golfing buddy. Ron looked less surprised than I did, so I quickly surmised that at least one of us had been let in on Seth's plan. Promising myself to skewer Seth later and barbeque him in his own sauce, I smiled and gave Ron the once-over. Not bad. He was tall and nicely built, even good-looking in a bland, guy-next-door sort of way. I was just thinking what a nice first impression he made when he opened his mouth and ruined it.

"So that wreck out front is yours?" he began. "Hey, you oughta come down to the dealership. I'll make you a great deal on something worth driving. I'm the top salesman they have, you know." I tried to fake a pleasant smile.

By the time Denise had brought the last dish from the kitchen, Seth had taken the ribs off the barbeque, and the four of us had rounded up all four kids at the dining room table, I already knew that Ron had played quarterback at the U, that he surely would have been drafted by the NFL were it not for the tragic accident that had blown out his left knee early in his senior season, and that he was "by far" the best sales rep at a nearby auto mall, where he would be happy to take care of me anytime I wanted to get rid of the trash heap I had parked out front and get a real car. (I grimaced at that second shot to my vehicle, but Ron, who by then had proven that he could maintain the same speaking pace even with a mouthful of barbequed ribs, didn't notice.) Before we got to dessert, I'd heard about every major, game-winning play he'd made since high school, how he hadn't served a mission because he could serve so much better in professional sports, and exactly—I mean exactly, to the penny—how much his last paycheck had been, including the bonus he had earned for being "New Employee of the Month." That was when I pushed back my chair, thanked Seth and Denise for the dinner, forced another smile as I told Ron it had been nice to meet him (inwardly repenting for the lie), and started for the coat closet.

"Don't you want dessert?" Denise asked, but her sympathetic expression said she didn't blame me for getting out of there.

"No thanks," I answered. "I'm avoiding unnecessary fat just now."

Denise slapped a hand over her mouth to stifle a giggle.

"As I was saying," Ron began, turning to face Seth as he launched into another football story.

Seth said, "We'll call you," and gave me the same sympathetic look I'd just earned from his wife. I scowled at him over the back of Ron's head.

As the door shut behind me, I could hear Ron saying, "You've really got to get her down to the dealership. That junk heap she's driving is going to fall apart any day now."

As I climbed into the "junk heap," grateful to be getting out of there before my brain homogenized, I realized that Ron had not asked or learned a single thing about me. In fact, I'd struggled to get a word in once in awhile. So much for Seth's matchmaking abilities. I resolved to ask what he had in mind before I accepted another invitation.

Unfortunately, I didn't think to apply that new rule to my brother Tim, who called the next day to ask me to Friday dinner at his house. I love all my nieces and nephews, but I have a special soft spot for Tim, Jr. He was born with a ventricular septal defect, an extra hole in his heart, and we had spent the first two years of his life praying for him with every blessing on the food and fasting for him at least once every month. Sure enough, the Lord had blessed us, the defect had grown closed, and Timmy, now almost four, was a beautiful child, a bundle of energy, a regular Mr. Personality. His little sister, two-year-old Elise, was a darling, too—all blond curls and cuddles. I always loved my visits at Tim and Wendy's.

Perhaps that was why I was surprised all over again to discover that Wendy had invited a man she knew from her music class at the community college. He was a production manager from a local company that made orthopedic hardware, and he, like Wendy, had recently been called as music chairperson for his ward and was trying to polish his skills.

Mick, short for Michael, wasn't as good-looking as Ron, but (and thank goodness!) he wasn't nearly as full of himself, either. We actually carried on something of a conversation during dinner—that is, if you can call this a conversation:

Me: So Mick, I understand you know Wendy through a music class?

Him: That's right.

Me: And you're learning to lead music?

Him: Yep.

Me: And how's that going?

Him: Great.

Long pause.

Me: Great. So, uh, your company makes orthopedic hardware, right?

Him: Um-hm.

The awkward silence was almost a pleasant change after Ron's one-sided chatter, but by the time Wendy was ready to serve dessert, I was fully aware that dating Mick would be hard work—harder than I felt up for. Skipping dessert once again, I thanked Tim and Wendy for the meal, kissed Timmy and Elise good-bye, and said "Nice to have met you" to Mick without having to cross my fingers. Then I climbed back into the trash heap and got out of there, wondering what Wendy had seen in Mick that she thought would work for me.

* * *

Someone in my family must have designated October as "Set Up Sarah Month." I'd hardly had time to put the Ron and Mick experiences behind me when Deb called on Saturday morning from the mall up the road. She said she was picking out new school shoes for Brittan, my oldest niece who had just turned ten, and needed my opinion. I was sharp enough to recognize she just wanted my company and to even feel a little flattered. I never thought to suspect her of matchmaking.

Derek was tall and had the Nordic good looks I associated with Brian's family, which made sense as soon as Deb introduced him as Brian's cousin Derek. He was pleasant and kind, good with the children, and interesting to talk to. During the next half hour, we took the three younger kids to get ice cream while my pregnant sister helped Brittan buy shoes.

"So you served your mission in Venezuela," I said as we walked. Keeping the kids together was harder than I had thought it would be. It might have been easier to teach geese to dance. "What part?"

"Best mission in the Church," he answered, herding Ryan back toward the group. "Maracaibo."

"No kidding! My brother Noah served there. You didn't happen to know an Elder Kimball, did you?"

"No," he paused to pull Maren out from behind a pillar, "but I did hear about him. He must have left just before I got there. My trainer had been his companion a few months before."

"Small world," I said, marveling at just how often that happened in the Church. "Hey, Nolan, stop teasing your sister!"

After we ordered the cones, the kids sat still long enough to eat their ice cream while Derek told me about the small appliance shop he was buying in Orem and his calling as the elders quorum president in his ward. As we started herding the kids back toward Deb and Brittan, he asked about my school class and listened with apparent interest as I bragged about my third graders.

We were hitting it off well, and I was just beginning to think that having a relative set me up might not always be a bad thing when Derek said, "Look, I don't know what Deborah had in mind by introducing us like this, but I think you ought to know . . ." He then went on to tell me about the "wonderful girl" who worked with him in the appliance shop and how he was planning to propose. I congratulated him and gave myself a mental pat on the back for not having said or done anything to make a fool of myself.

Later that day, when Deb called to ask how I liked Cousin Derek, I suggested she ask him about his marriage plans. "And while you're at it," I added, "could you *please* tell the rest of the family not to set me up anymore?"

Deb laughed and apologized, promising she'd spread the word.

Apparently word didn't get to Josh and Barbara, who called the next week to say they were driving up on Friday and would I like to go to dinner? Color me dense. I didn't even think to ask who else might be coming. Evan came to the door with Josh when they picked me up.

He was pleasant—pleasant to look at, pleasant to talk to, pleasant to be around. There wasn't anything dynamic or different about him, but I enjoyed that first dinner enough to let him drive me home that evening, at which time I agreed to go out with him again. The second date was pleasant, too—though I saw hints he might be feeling possessive. He tended to hover just a little too close and kept one hand lightly on my back or arm at all times. It wasn't enough to cause me real discomfort, but it did cause the "Warning! Potential problem here!" light to go off in my head. When he asked for a third date, I hesitated just a little before I said, "Um, yeah. Sure."

When Evan said he'd pick me up the next evening at seven, I assumed we were going to a fireside somewhere, so I wore a light dress and a sweater. I wasn't prepared for a walk around the temple grounds, which was exactly where Evan drove us—and not to the Jordan River Temple, either, which is less than two miles from my home. He drove us into downtown, then spent nearly twenty minutes hunting for street parking next to Temple Square.

"I'm really not dressed for the weather, Evan," I said, trying to be kind. "It's awfully cold out there, and I just have a light sweater."

Evan smiled benignly. "We won't be here long," he said, then slipped into a parallel parking space just as a compact pulled out. His full-size sedan barely fit into the tiny space, but we were close enough to Temple Square that I decided I probably wouldn't die—if we didn't stay more than three minutes.

A few light flakes were starting to fall as we walked up to the back side of the lighted Salt Lake Temple and stopped beside the flagpole. Although I was hugging myself and keeping my lips closed so my teeth wouldn't chatter out loud, I still savored the peaceful spirit one feels on holy ground, so it wasn't as bad as it could have been. When Evan dropped to one knee in front of me, I thought he was stopping to tie his shoe.

"N-need help?" I asked through the chattering.

"Well, yes, in a manner of speaking." He cleared his throat.

I swear I didn't know what was coming. If I had, I might have been able to contain my involuntary giggle. But when Evan pulled a ring box out of his pocket and asked me to marry him, I couldn't help myself. The situation was just too surreal.

"You're laughing at me," he said, his expression so wounded I felt horrible.

"No. No, honest, it's just . . ." I forced my face to compose itself. "Evan, you don't even know me."

He took my hand. "I know all I need to know. I'm surprised you haven't felt it too. It's just so obvious."

Had I missed something? "Excuse me, but *what* is so obvious?"

"Us," he said. "You and me. The energy between us. You're *the one*, Sarah. I knew it the moment I first saw you."

I bit my lip to keep the giggles from bubbling out again. Behind Evan's kneeling form, I could see a small group of teenaged girls gathering, probably Beehives and Mia Maids, presumably waiting for the tender moment when I accepted Evan's ring.

"Evan, get up," I said, tugging on his coat sleeve.

"What?"

"Get up!" I whispered loudly, now with some urgency.

"But you haven't answered—"

"Please, Evan." The girls near the Tabernacle were starting to giggle.

His expression hardened. "I never imagined you could be so cruel." Stiff with anger, Evan stood, closing the ring box with a loud snap, and stalked back toward the gate through which we had entered. I had to run to catch up.

"Evan, please listen. You don't understand." I hadn't wanted to hurt him. I just wanted him to get up off his knee and stop embarrassing us both. But there wasn't any adequate way to apologize for the fact that I hadn't accepted his proposal, and I wasn't about to marry him just to calm his hurt feelings. For goodness' sake, the man was a stranger! He drove me home in sullen silence and watched from behind the wheel while I entered my front door. That was the last time I ever saw Evan.

* * *

By the following week, I had been surprised twice more—once by one of Mark's former companions, who had promised my brother he would look me up when he got home, and a second time by my friend Jeanie, who called from her home in Denver to tell me about a nice friend of her husband's who happened to be living "just up the road" from me in West Jordan. I tried to be polite to everyone involved, but by Halloween, when even my eighty-year-old neighbor had tried to set me up with a friend of her grandson's, I had just about had all the good intentions I could take.

For the second month in a row, I was the last to arrive at my parents' home for our fast Sunday dinner, and the family was getting impatient. There was some good-natured banter as we all settled into our accustomed places, but some of it seemed rather pointed, like Josh's whispered comment about "not knowing a good thing when she sees it." He was grinning when he said it, but I wasn't quite convinced. If he thought I was desperate enough to marry a man I'd known less than a day . . .

"Sarah, will you please—" my father began, and the tension that had been gathering for the past month blew.

"WILL THIS FAMILY PLEASE STOP TRYING TO RUN MY LIFE?" I shouted at the top of my lungs.

The entire Kimball clan stared in stunned silence. I was aghast, horrified at myself. I don't think I'd ever screamed at my family in my entire life.

"Are you all right, Sarah?" my mother asked, her voice tentative.

"I was just going to ask if you'd say the prayer," my father murmured, his voice barely audible.

"I'm fine," I said, but the tears coursing down both cheeks probably suggested otherwise. "That is, I will be." I stood and pushed my chair in. "Please, go ahead without me." Then I ran from the room.

By the time I'd composed myself and was ready to return to the table, the mood in the dining room was still subdued but more or less back to normal. I stood at the front of the table, next to my father's chair, prepared to eat crow. "I want to apologize to everyone—" I began, but my father cut me off.

"Sit down, Sarah," he said, gently taking my hand. "You're the one who is owed an apology." He nodded toward Deborah.

"I'm sorry, sis," Deb said. "I meant well, but I had no right to interfere."

"Me too," said Josh. "I just wanted to see you happy."

"I'm *really* sorry about Ron," Seth said.

"You should be!" I said. Then I giggled. That broke the tension. Tim's apology got squeezed in between the other comments as the family laughed and told horror stories about everyone's attempts to find Sarah a man. By the time things had settled down and I had actually started my dinner, I remembered why I loved all these snoopy, meddling, interfering relatives of mine. And when Ruth reminded me that I could have done better if I'd tried her computer dating service, I didn't even mind—much.

That evening after our family visit had ended, I walked out to my car, buoyed up by the thought that it might be safe to get back into the gene pool. However, my happy bubble burst when I went out to climb into my faithful "trash heap," only to have it fulfill all of Ron's evil prophecies. It not only stalled halfway down the block but actually fell apart, right there on the road. I walked back to the house and explained what had happened. Dad, Josh, Seth, and Noah walked back with me (Tim had already left, or he'd have been there, too). We made a sad spectacle, standing in the street beside my dead car, doing a cursory post-mortem as the neighbors drove around us, asking if we needed help.

"Looks like it threw a rod," Josh said. (In truth, Josh wouldn't know a rod if it transformed into a snake like Moses' staff and bit him, but I wasn't about to say that, since I wouldn't know it, either.)

"I'd say it probably crashed the bell housing," Dad said, his head under the hood.

"One thing's for sure, Sarah." It was Noah, sounding the death knell to my old jalopy. "You're not going to be driving this old junker anymore."

I gulped. "I only live a couple of miles from the school," I said, trying to be brave. "I guess I can walk."

"Sarah, it's at least two miles," Josh began.

"You will borrow your mom's car," Dad said, his voice putting an end to the discussion. "You're welcome to use it until you've found yourself something else to drive. Come on, guys. Let's get this heap out of the road."

They pushed aside the pile of metal that had been my independence an hour before. Suddenly I had worse problems than my family trying to set me up. My very last dollar had gone into buying my home, and my teacher's salary was already stretching like a waistband on Thanksgiving. "How am I going to buy a car?" I mumbled.

"The Lord provides," my mother said, sliding her arm around my shoulders. Until that moment, I hadn't even realized she was there.

I couldn't bring myself to write much in my journal that night. My entry for the day read, "My car is dead, but my family still loves me." Thank heaven I still had the Kimballs!

Chapter 3

When it comes to car shopping, the word that comes to my mind is *ordeal.* I know there are people who enjoy it, but there are also people who stick pins in their eyelids and walk on hot coals. Luckily, my dad knew just how I felt, having shopped with me for the one car I had bought just three years ago. Before I left him that Sunday, he'd stuck a business card in my hand and said, "Ask for Pat." That's how I found myself at one of the major car dealerships in the valley Monday evening, waiting for Pat. (Hint: If you're shopping for a car in the Salt Lake Valley, go on Monday evening. You can get plenty of quiet, personalized attention.)

It would be tough to describe the trepidation I felt as I waited. First, I was shopping in a place that had always terrified me—the used-car section. I remembered my Aunt Lizbeth, who was single at the time, declaring that she'd no sooner buy a used car than marry a divorced man. "Why," she asked, "would I want someone else's problems?" That made perfect sense to me, but since I couldn't afford to buy *any* car, I felt it would be doubly irresponsible to look at *new* cars, so I confined myself to the back of the lot.

My second reason for being so ill at ease was simple: I was expecting a Ron-clone who would not only try to intimidate me into buying much more car than I could possibly afford, but would probably also talk down to me when I didn't understand engine sizes or try to sell me based on the placement of my vanity mirrors.

Imagine my relief when Pat turned out to be Patricia, a charming, poised, thoroughly helpful woman in her mid-thirties who not only refused to push but actually listened when I described what I wanted and didn't want in a car. Within a rather pleasant two-hour span, I had found a little car I really liked—even though it was used. The deal Pat arranged had payments that I could actually qualify for, though I still wasn't sure how I'd afford them. Since Dad had managed to have my dead clunker towed to a parts yard and had miraculously come away with a little cash, I was even able to make a small down payment. By the time I went home again Monday evening, I had a "new" car.

I also had a new payment to make, which didn't figure into my budget at all. All that week, I pondered how to make ends meet. Then the following Saturday morning, Ruth came by to help me paint the front hallway, and I found myself explaining my finances as we rolled Rock Candy White onto the walls.

"Sounds like you've got two choices," Ruth said. "Either cut expenses or increase your income."

"Gee. I wouldn't have thought of that."

Ruth ignored the sarcasm. "Have you thought of renting out a room?"

"You mean, take in boarders?"

Ruth snorted. "I was thinking more along the lines of taking in a roommate, but you could run a boarding house if you like."

"Oh." When I'd bought the house, I'd been engaged and planning to build a family with Kyle, so I hadn't thought of looking for a roommate. I didn't know why the thought hadn't occurred to me earlier. "Do you think that could work?"

"Of course it *could* work. The question is *would* it, and you won't know that until you try."

"Umm, right," I answered.

"Just like you should try this dating service," Ruth said, sensing a weakening in my position.

I held up a finger and flashed my warning look. "Don't even go there."

We finished the hallway quickly—it was a small space—and I called for pizza while we washed up the brushes. Later, we sat in the kitchen gorging on the all-veggie special and looking through the ads in a local throwaway shopper that was faithfully delivered every Thursday morning by a cute little red-haired kid on a bike.

I turned first to the "Room for Rent" classifieds, figuring I'd check out the competition and get some idea of what rooms in our area were going for. Ruth picked up another section of the paper. I thought she might be looking at weekend shoe sales and felt a little miffed that she wasn't being more helpful. That's when she said, "Listen to this!" It turned out Ruth had found a column for people who were looking for rooms.

Aloud she read, "Wanted: Room for female student with two-year-old daughter and well-mannered cat."

"I dunno," I said immediately. "A single mother? What would I be getting myself into? Child custody issues? Word of Wisdom problems?"

"Stop being so prejudiced. You never know until you check it out," Ruth answered, and showed me the ad.

The prospective renter had listed the price she was willing to pay—an amount somewhat lower than was listed in most of the ads I'd just been reading but reasonably competitive—and had given a local phone number.

"The rent she's offering really isn't much," I said.

"She probably doesn't have much," Ruth answered. "What do you suppose she means by 'well-mannered'?"

In the end it was curiosity about the well-mannered cat that got me, and I found myself dialing the number. The woman who answered identified herself as Shari Crawford. When she said she'd just about given up on finding anything in her price range, I hesitated, wondering if I was cheating myself out of a few extra bucks but knowing the amount she was offering would cover my car payment, plus a little extra. Besides, the longer we talked, the more curious I felt—about her, her child, why she was single, her well-mannered cat . . . Minutes later, Shari was knocking at my door.

She had her daughter, Kerry, with her, and I was charmed from the beginning by the toddler, even if I still felt a little wary about the mother. We Kimballs make pretty babies, and there were currently four in our family—yet as adorable as they all were, none was more appealing than little Kerry, who stared in wide-eyed wonder at everything in my tiny, spare little home as if she were touring the queen's pavilion. It was both humbling and touching.

"This is nice," Shari said, though I could tell she was trying to contain her enthusiasm. Maybe she thought I'd raise the rent if I saw how much she wanted, or needed, this space. "Do you have *two* rooms available?" she asked, looking down my hallway.

I started to say yes, since I was only using one of my three bedrooms, but Ruth shook her head, reminding me that anytime she came up for the weekend, she'd need a place to stay. "No, just the one," I said, "but it's large."

"It is," Shari agreed, inspecting it again. "Now, about the cat—"

"What do you mean by well-mannered?"

It turned out that Shari and Kerry owned a neutered tabby cat named Harry, after Harry Potter. "We thought we'd give him a magical name, since he seems able to appear and disappear at will," Shari explained. "He's very clean, though, and never fights. He doesn't need a cat box if he has a way to get outside, and—"

"I don't know how I'd feel about having a cat door," I said, thinking of a piece I'd heard on the news about an elderly couple who had been robbed by a contortionist.

"He's an excellent mouser," Shari went on, which reminded me of the flash of gray fur I'd seen two days before when getting into my new car in my old garage.

"We can always give it a try," I answered, though I was still a bit wary of the whole situation.

At that point, events seemed to take on a life of their own, and by mid-afternoon, we'd found a rental contract in a local office supply store and had arranged for Shari, Kerry, and Harry to move in after school the next Monday. Noah showed up an hour later to install a ready-made cat door between the kitchen and the garage, and another between the garage and the outside. I took Shari's first check to the bank, waiting, just in case, until the teller assured me there were sufficient funds to cover it.

Despite some serious misgivings, I had felt comfortable being around Shari. Still, just to cover my bases, I called all her references that afternoon while Noah was working on the cat doors. All of them talked about what a good person and fine mother she was, and how she'd gotten a rotten deal in her divorce. One of Shari's references, her bishop, assured me that my renting to her would be an answer to a prayer. That was enough for me.

After the check was cashed and the cat doors were finished, Noah, Ruth, and I munched on the leftover pizza and speculated about what it would be like to have a two-year-old and a cat in the house. It wasn't long until the conversation turned back to Ruth's new favorite subject.

"You really should try Mormons2Marry.com," she began.

"Why are you pushing this so hard?"

"Because I've seen it work," Ruth said. "You remember me telling you about my roommate's older sister?"

"The hopelessly awkward woman with buckteeth and bad skin?"

"Yeah, that one. She used this dating service, and she's married now."

"Ugh. Thanks for the comparison."

"Oh, come on, Sarah. You know I didn't mean—"

"Sorry, sis, but I'm not that desperate." I waved a slice of cold pizza.

"I don't consider it desperation," Noah said. "I've already been on my first date."

"You're kidding." True, for me computer-arranged dates held all the charm of a train wreck, but people stare at train wrecks, too. "So how'd it go?"

"Not bad. I don't think I'm going to see her again, though. Her idea of what constitutes a 'slight age difference' seems to be different from mine."

Ruth chuckled, and I tried to keep a straight face. "Not exactly a sweet young thing?" I asked.

"Well, I stopped short of asking her if Moses really had a long beard," Noah admitted, and we all laughed.

"I don't get it," I said as the giggles subsided. "Didn't you see her picture before you met her?"

"You're thinking of a different dating service," Ruth said, "the one where you just throw your picture and personal description out on the airwaves, and anyone who pays the few bucks to buy a password can check you out."

I raised an eyebrow. "I thought that's what you were talking about."

"Oh, no. This is much more discreet," Noah answered, and he proceeded to describe just how Ruth's favorite dating service worked. Apparently this service, which cost a bit more than the first, required the new member to fill out two lengthy questionnaires: one describing himself or herself, and the other describing the potential mate. The computer then ran the comparisons against each other and e-mailed each member a list of "best match" possibilities, using code names and e-mail addresses only. After that, it was up to each client to follow through, but the service recommended that their clients share no more personal information until after they had met in a public place. I was impressed by the agency's efforts at client protection.

"So have you contacted anyone else?" I asked Noah.

"Not yet," he answered. "I just met Heidi for lunch today. I thought I'd let that cool for a couple of days before I tried again with someone else."

"Sounds wise," Ruth said. There was silence at the table for a full twenty seconds, then Ruth burst into laughter, followed quickly by Noah and me.

"Aren't we a sad lot," Noah said, "planning dating strategies while we hang out with our sibs on a Saturday night."

"Absolutely tragic," I agreed, shaking my head, though I couldn't stop laughing. "More pizza, anyone?" To cement our shared nerdiness, we ended the evening with a rousing game of Scrabble, and I threw Noah out by 10:00 P.M., since I had an early meeting the next morning.

I really did intend to go to sleep early, too, but long after Noah had gone and Ruth had retired to the guest room for the night, long after completing my journal entry and saying my prayers, I still lay awake, wondering what it would be like to share my home with Shari and her odd little family. And, even though I didn't want to admit it, I was starting to wonder if maybe Mormons2Marry.com was worth a try.

* * *

Shari moved in on Monday afternoon. Noah and Tim showed up to help, and there were a couple of harried hours while Kerry found her way into every nook and cranny in my little house, and Harry discovered even more. By the time I fed both my brothers and my new housemates from a pot of homemade corn chowder, Shari's few things were put away, Kerry was ready to go down for the night, and Harry was quietly purring in a basket in the corner. Tim excused himself for family home evening with Wendy and the kids, and Noah left right behind him. With Kerry tucked into bed, Shari and I sat down to get acquainted. We started with the tale of her divorce.

"I married for all the right reasons, and Ken married for all the wrong ones," Shari said simply. "He was a returned missionary and a priesthood holder and he took me to the temple, but none of that seemed to matter after a few months."

"How'd it end?" I asked, suddenly understanding why I had felt so comfortable with my new roomie, despite my previous concerns. Her experience with Ken was much like mine with Kyle.

"It sounds like a soap opera," Shari said with a wry half smile. "He was driving me home from the hospital after Kerry was born when he told me he'd been seeing another woman for nearly a year and had spent the last four days since my cesarean at her house."

I gasped. "The jerk! Did he ask for a divorce right there in the car?"

"I wish." Shari sipped at a cup of peppermint tea. "He told me he felt I deserved to know how things stood but that he'd really like to keep everything just the way it was."

I choked on my orange juice. "You're kidding! He actually expected you to approve of him having an affair?"

"Not just approve." Shari nodded. "He wanted me to acknowledge her as a member of our family, even welcome her into my home."

"Oh, Shari."

"I didn't stay long after that."

"No, I don't imagine." I paused. "I didn't stay long after I heard about Kyle's other woman, either."

Shari looked around. "I wondered if you got the house in a divorce."

"No divorce," I said quickly. "We were engaged. Six weeks before the wedding, on the very day I had scheduled to address the invitations with my mom, Kyle showed up to tell me about a girl from his hometown in Missouri. It seemed he'd spent 'a lot of time' with her when he was home over the summer."

"Did he tell you he'd fallen out of love with you?"

"Not really. It was more complicated than that . . ." I trailed off.

"Oh, no," Shari said, guessing the rest. "She was pregnant, and he felt he had to marry her."

I nodded. "Exactly. That was even the phrase he used, 'I *have* to marry her, honey. Her dad is my dad's boss, and well, you understand how it is,'" I whined as I mimicked Kyle. A poor impersonation was the least he deserved.

"Ouch," Shari said, wincing. "So you bought the house as a consolation prize?"

"Not quite. After Kyle proposed, he wanted to take me shopping for a ring. I suggested we use the money for a down payment instead. Then, because he didn't have enough to make the whole down payment on this place, I cleaned out my savings account. I still had some cash left from an insurance settlement from a bad car accident back in high school."

"Oh, no! Are you okay?"

I nodded, appreciating that Shari seemed to care. "Yeah. I almost died at the time, but my dad gave me a blessing, and the whole ward—not to mention my whole family—all fasted and prayed for me. I recovered completely, but the insurance company still paid a settlement, which helped me with school—"

"—and with buying this place," Shari finished.

I nodded again. "Of course, after Kyle decided he 'had' to marry Beth, he wanted his money back, but I was hurt and angry, and the title to the house was in my name, since it was supposed to be an engagement gift. I pushed the closing date through as fast as I could. Kyle threatened to sue—"

"No! How awful!"

"But when I pointed out the fact that I could sue him for breach of contract, he let the whole thing drop."

"Did he marry the girl—uh, Beth?"

I felt my throat constrict as I recalled reading the announcement in the newspaper. "Yeah. A couple of weeks after he told me about her. They were married in the cultural hall of the Hazelwood Ward, near St. Louis."

"I think I understand how you must feel," Shari said. "I felt I was the wronged party when I left Ken—"

"You were!"

"But I came out of the divorce with less than I'd taken into the marriage—except for Kerry." She grinned, and I could see how much she adored her baby. "I was awarded child support for Kerry, of course, but it comes late, when it comes at all. Mostly I'm living on the generosity of my family, occasional help from Church welfare, and student loans until I finish my teaching credential."

"Oh? What is it you're planning to teach?"

"Probably the primary grades."

"Did I mention I teach third grade?"

"No! Really?"

Our conversation shifted gears as Shari and I shared ideas about the teaching profession and what was wrong with schools these days. By the time we finally forced ourselves to go to bed, I knew I'd made a good choice in renting to Shari.

We all adjusted quickly. Shari and I chatted into the evening so often that we had to create a self-imposed curfew just to get some sleep. As we drew near the Thanksgiving season, Shari and Kerry already felt like part of my family—Shari like a third sister, Kerry like another darling niece, and even Harry seemed to belong there. (The down side to this was that he chose to treat me just like I was part of *his* family; I got up one morning to find the lower half of a lizard still wriggling on my kitchen counter.) This wasn't the match I'd been hoping to find, and it obviously wasn't an eternal answer for any of us, but Shari and her family filled a gap in my life, as well as helping me pay for my car, and I felt real thanksgiving as we approached the holiday.

I found myself reflecting on an experience I'd had some three or four years earlier, when I was doing lower-division work at BYU. I had been in a humanities class that had me attending all the art exhibits in the Harris Fine Arts Center. One day in the HFAC, I had seen a show staged as one artist's final project for the master of fine arts degree. It had changed my perception of the Savior and my relationship to Him.

I was struck by the delicate beauty of all the paintings in that MFA show; each one was a lift to my spirit. The artist had an uncanny way of capturing the sense of a background in impressionistic or abstract ways, yet the human figures—and especially the figure of the Savior—were always so photographically lifelike, it almost seemed they'd be warm to the touch.

One painting spoke to me even more than the others. The background suggested spring grasses and flowers, and the colors were vivid and beautiful, but that wasn't what struck me most. In the painting, a young woman close to my own age was running toward the Savior, her arms outstretched, her face hopeful. He was walking toward her, His arms reaching out to take her in, and He was smiling the most wonderful, accepting, and loving smile. The painting was titled *Embrace,* and ever since I had first seen it, I had called it to mind whenever I needed to feel close to my Savior.

I know this might not sound like a very profound experience to some, but to me it was. Since I was a child, I'd been impressed by the *duty* part of being a member of the Church, by the responsibility to follow all the Lord's commandments and to try to do as many good works as one could squeeze into a day. I guess you could say I was motivated by fear, although I never thought of it that way. Somehow, whenever I'd tried to imagine the Savior, I had pictured Him as the carpenter who suffered on the cross, anguished and sorrowing, or the Eternal Lawgiver, stern and disapproving. The artist at the MFA show pictured Him as warm and loving, even laughing, often surrounded by little children, and I suddenly realized that a true Christian should be motivated by love, not duty.

As I knelt to say my prayers that Sunday before Thanksgiving, my mind called up these images, and I could see myself running into the Savior's arms. I wanted to tell Him how much I appreciated all He had done for me and how blessed I felt to have Shari's little family in my home. And then, with even greater gratitude, I realized that prayer itself was one of the greatest blessing in my life. No matter what my circumstances, I would never be alone.

Chapter 4

We Kimballs have always been good at birthdays. With ten of us in the household, we didn't dare spend a lot, but we always gathered the family together and made an occasion of it. Mom cooked the birthday person's favorite dinner, Dad recited a cheesy little saying about birthdays from the head of the table, and family members pitched in with gifts that were short on expense but long on thought and caring. Mark once gave Ruth a whole *month* of making her bed and shining her Sunday shoes. He followed through with it, too. For us, birthdays were about caring.

That was the case when it came to everyone but me, anyway. It's not that I'm complaining, mind you . . . Well, okay, maybe I *am* complaining, but it should be against the creed of Nature to deliver a baby during Thanksgiving week, or during any other major holiday for that matter. Everybody else in the family got great birthdays, isolated from other celebrations. Dad's is in late January, and Mom's is in August. Tim always had pool parties for his birthday in August, and Deb, Josh, and Seth got cupcakes at school for their birthdays in April and September. So did Noah, who has a birthday in early May, as well as Mark and Ruth, with their spring birthdays. I'm the odd one out in the Kimball family, born on November twenty-first. I think that birthday is great—now that I'm older—but when I was a kid, I always felt short-changed, as if my birthday got ignored in the midst of the larger (though clearly less important) celebration. My journals from my fifth- and sixth-grade years are particularly angry about it. Then again, the entries for those years are particularly angry about almost everything.

Since my birthday often hits during Thanksgiving week, Mom and I made a treaty to celebrate annually on the Saturday after the holiday. One of my favorite meals ever is curried turkey (served over brown rice—yum!), which makes it easy on Mom, who cooks an enormous bird and always has plenty of leftovers. On that one day of the holiday weekend, we eat birthday cake instead of pie, and no one is allowed to turn on TV football until I've blown out my candles. These are small compromises, but during my teen years, they kept me from staging a full-scale mutiny and demanding that my birthday be celebrated halfway 'round the year, which is how my friend Jeanie dealt with her Christmas Eve birthday. Her family celebrates on June 24.

Anyway, at some point I began to care less about birthdays and even to foresee a time when I'd be just as happy to have them pass unnoticed. Still, the Saturday-after-Thanksgiving tradition continues, and family members have learned to count on curried turkey and birthday cake two days after the usual feast. So when November twenty-first came on the Tuesday before Thanksgiving, it didn't feel like my birthday. In fact, I hardly noticed it.

My third graders, anticipating the long weekend, were antsier than usual, and I spent much of the day refereeing a sniping match between Lillian and Ellen Brenner. Ellen's quips were much more devastating, of course, but blessedly, Lillian wasn't sharp enough to notice, so they managed to end on more or less equal terms, leaving me grateful but exhausted and hoping they'd manage to settle things before the next morning.

I decided to grade the math papers and spelling quizzes at school rather than take them with me, and I was feeling fairly battered by the time I slunk home, ready to collapse. I arrived to find the house smelling heavenly and dinner on the table, even though it was my week to cook.

As I finished my last bite of chicken cacciatore and pushed my plate away, thanking Shari for the wonderful food, she produced a beautifully wrapped box with a big bow.

"What—? Oh, my birthday! How did you know?"

"Noah clued me in."

"Then remind me to thank Noah." I opened the box, admiring the loveliest, softest, orchid-pink angora sweater I'd ever seen. I hugged Shari, then said, "I can't keep it, you know. It must have cost a fortune! You don't have that kind of mon—"

"You just have to know how to shop," she assured me. "I found it at D.I., but it's new. Look, the tags are still on."

"So you really *can* afford it?" I asked, already guilty of coveting it.

"I already have." She grinned.

"Great! I'll wear it to Thanksgiving dinner."

But I couldn't wait that long. I wore it the next day with a pair of charcoal-colored wool slacks and strolled into school feeling attractive for the first time in months. More than one of my male colleagues, and even a few of the fathers, gave me appreciative glances as I walked toward my classroom. Our custodian—Brother Hartgraves, who used to be my Sunday School teacher—whistled when he saw me, and even Joey Turley said, "You look pretty today, Miss Kimball." I left that afternoon feeling energized despite the ongoing war between the Brenner twins. I was thanking Shari all over again that evening at dinner when the phone rang.

It was Noah. "Hi, sis. Just wanted to ask you about dinner tomorrow . . ."

We'd been talking about Thanksgiving dinner for the last couple of weeks. With Shari and Kerry joining the usual Kimball gathering (her parents were going to her brother's place in Alaska), and a couple of sibs-in-law bringing relatives, we'd had to arrange to borrow a table and chairs from my parents' ward building. Setting up such a large dinner for so many of us was akin to taking on the logistical challenges of feeding the Sixth Army. "So what's new?" I asked.

Noah told me about Justin Owen, a former missionary companion now finishing his engineering degree at BYU. "He's too far away from his family in Florida to fly home for the weekend, so I invited him to join us, but I didn't want you to think it was a setup, so, well . . . I guess I'm asking for permission. Is it okay with you if Justin joins us at Thanksgiving?"

"Heavens, Noah! Of course!" Had I really become such a shrew that my brother had to ask permission for an act of Christian kindness? "Look, I'm sorry I've made you feel that way—"

"No problem," he assured. "I knew you'd be okay with it if you understood."

I winced and promised myself I'd make it up to everyone. "Noah? Thanks for telling Shari about my birthday. She got me the most gorgeous new sweater—"

"Wear it tomorrow," he said. There was a grin in his voice when he added, "You'll want to look nice for Justin."

"You skunk!" I said, but we both knew I was teasing. By the time I hung up, I was even a little curious about Noah's friend.

It turned out there was plenty about Justin to make him interesting. He had soft-looking brown hair with a few unruly little curls, a ready smile, and the sweetest puppy-dog brown eyes. Noah could have set me up with this one anytime he wanted to.

We all kind of seated ourselves at dinner that afternoon, but somehow I ended up sitting across from Justin, and I've got to admit I rather liked the way he looked at me. It made me glad I'd worn the new sweater. Noah, who ended up seated several places down from us, across from Shari, kept looking from Justin to me and back to Justin and raising his eyebrows. Somehow I managed to ignore him.

Justin and I got acquainted over dinner, and I learned more about his family in Florida (he was one of six kids) and his major in engineering (he hoped to design supersonic jets someday). He showed interest in me, too, and I told him about Lillian and Ellen and the sociology experiment in sibling rivalry they had been conducting in my classroom. He laughed and observed that sisters could be that way—then saw my look and added that brothers were pretty good at it, too. How could I *not* like a guy like that?

For some families, Thanksgiving is about the turkey; for others, it's about football. In Kimball family tradition, it's about the pie. We always have at least two dozen of them, and while there are favorites (pumpkin, apple, and cherry are always on the menu, along with lemon meringue and at least one pecan—Seth's favorite), we try out new recipes every year. Given the emphasis on dessert, there is always a couple of hours' pause between the meal and the pie—we like to let the appetizers settle before we start in on the main course.

During the wait before serving the pie, we have our annual name drawing. As holiday traditions go, this is one of the newer ones for our family, started some ten or twelve years ago when the older kids were teens. That's about when they discovered that it could get expensive to purchase nice gifts for every family member and that there was little charm to gifts purchased for under two dollars each. Since then we've drawn for names.

The ritual starts when Dad takes a slip of paper with each sibling's name on it and puts them all in his baseball cap with the Jazz logo on the front. Then, starting with Deb, who's oldest, each Kimball sibling draws the name of another. The only time we put the name back is if we draw our own or if the last person does. Whatever name we draw, that's the one person—or family—for whom we buy Christmas gifts. It saves on everyone's hard-earned cash but allows us to give nicer gifts.

As the time for this year's drawing came, Dad tossed all our names in his Jazz hat and started around the circle. Seth drew his own name and had to draw again, and then I drew Seth for the second year in a row. With that, Thanksgiving dinner was officially over until the pie. I jumped in to help with cleanup and found myself working next to Justin, who fit in as easily as if he'd always been there.

Maybe it was his intuition as a mechanical engineer, but he helped us get the dirty work done in record time and even guessed how Mom liked to have her dishwasher loaded. I was impressed. So was Mom, and it was then that she intervened to do her own version of matchmaking.

"Sarah, why don't you show Justin the yard?" she said. I eagerly took the hint and slipped on a light jacket.

"Come on," I said. "I'll show you the tree house where Noah broke his arm when he was seven."

"Only because you pushed me," Noah called from behind us, but I noticed he didn't leave the football game, where most of the guys were ensconced.

"That is, unless you'd rather watch the game," I said as we stepped outside.

"My team's not playing, anyway."

I raised my eyebrows.

"Dolphins fan," he explained with a shrug. "Now let's see that tree house."

We walked for awhile, and I showed him the tree house, the garden, and the climbing bars Dad had put in when we were kids. He talked a little about his family in Orlando, and I liked him better all the time. As we edged sideways into the narrow space where Noah, Ruth, Mark, and I had often slipped through the fence to walk to school, he stood very close, and I realized he wasn't much taller than I was. He would only have to duck a couple of inches to bring his puppy-dog eyes level with mine. I shivered with awareness and ducked out of sight. He followed, and we walked toward the elementary school.

When we came to the point where we had to cross the big ditch, Justin took my hand to help me jump over it, then held it just as naturally as if we'd been walking that way forever. We strolled like that all the way to the school. I showed him around to the various school rooms and talked about some of the family lore connected to our school, then we sat side by side on the sixth-grader swings (the ones that didn't have safety latches on the seats) and chatted some more while we idly drifted in the afternoon breeze.

It wasn't until I suddenly shivered that I realized how much time had passed; the sun was already lowering in the sky, and the family had probably started serving pie without us—which gave me some idea of just how much I'd been enjoying Justin's company. He took my hand again as we strolled back toward the house (this time, taking the longer street route), and we were still holding hands as we walked up to the front door.

Brittan was looking out the front window as we neared, and I knew that she had spread the word just by the speculative looks my family was giving us as we came in through the front door. Thank goodness no one felt the need to say anything.

True to my prediction, the pies had already been cut, and at least seven empty pie plates were already stacked in the kitchen sink. "We'd better hurry before it's all gone," I said. "What's your pleasure?"

Justin didn't speak for a moment. Instead, he looked right at my lips and licked his own, giving me a slow, meaningful smile. Just as I felt the blush rising, he said, "Chocolate cream, I think."

"Right," I said, pretending nothing had happened, but my hand trembled as I cut into the chocolate cream, and I was finding it a bit difficult to catch my breath. "Do you, uh, want a full slice of chocolate, or would you like to try a little of something else, uh, some other pie as well?"

Justin stepped closer, looking at the pies. "I don't know. What else is good?" Although he was touching me now, his fingers resting gently at my elbow, his comment seemed to be reserved for dessert this time. Thank goodness! I was already weak in the knees.

I found my voice only slightly unsteady as I said, "My favorite is always the coconut cream, but I'm only going to have half a slice. That way I can try Deb's sour cream raisin, too."

"Yum. Sounds good. Give me half a chocolate cream and half a sour cream raisin."

"You've got it."

Somehow I served up four half slices of pie without dropping anything or embarrassing myself any further, and we took our plates to the table in the kitchen nook, which seemed to offer the only unoccupied seats in the house. We both ate slowly, sharing compliments for the pies and the cooks who had made them, and picking up bits and pieces of the conversations we'd shared in the past two or three hours. It was the most comfortable I'd felt with anyone since . . . I stopped the thought, unwilling to let Kyle into my warm afternoon.

The family card games started shortly after dessert—Hearts, Rook, and Uno, with a little more pie mixed in between rounds—and Justin and I were partners for a particularly satisfying round of One-High Rook, where we trounced Noah and Shari in only five hands. It was about then that I realized the disadvantage of riding over in the same car with my roommates. When Kerry began to cry and Shari announced it was almost her bedtime and we should probably be leaving, I realized that was my cue to leave the party.

Justin looked just as sad to see me getting ready to go as I felt to be going, but I made a point of inviting him to join us for my birthday dinner as I walked toward the entrance.

"It's your birthday Saturday?" he asked as I opened the door.

Kerry was crying full bore now, and Shari took her out, waving to everyone over her shoulder. "Not exactly," I answered. "Noah can explain it to you." Then I blew a few kisses to the family, said good-night to everyone, and hurriedly followed Shari to the car, expecting to share my newfound excitement with my roomie. I had expected her to be full of questions and speculation—you know, the typical roommate thing like you see on the movies—but even after she got

Kerry settled in her car seat, Shari merely talked about how delicious dinner had been and how fun the games were, then began humming a little tune under her breath. When we got home, I shared my excitement with my journal instead.

* * *

The weekend before, I'd made a date with Noah for lunch at my place on the day after Thanksgiving. By now he'd already had two of his made-in-computer-heaven dates, and that Friday morning he was meeting number three for breakfast, so I wanted a recap of the morning's events. Of course, I also found myself hoping he would bring Justin along, so I tried not to look disappointed when my brother arrived by himself. Shari had taken her daughter to see a college roommate who was visiting family for the holiday, so Noah and I had the house to ourselves. We chatted for a couple of minutes while I set the table and served up some linguine alfredo and green salad, then I asked Noah to bless it and we dug in to both the food and the day's topic.

"So tell me about it, Noah. Was this third date any better than the first two?" I passed him a roll and some butter.

"Yeah, it was," he answered. "She's a nice woman."

"No kidding. So you think you might see her again?"

He looked thoughtful. "I'm not sure, Sarah. I'm beginning to wonder if maybe you were right about this idea all along. I mean, maybe I'd do better if I just let it happen naturally and found my own dates."

"Okay. Now I'm confused. You like this woman, but you might not go out with her again?"

Noah gave me a long look, and I had the feeling he wanted to tell me something, but after a moment, he sighed and put his fork down. "I paid for five introductions. I guess I'm just trying to get my money's worth by meeting all five." He grinned at me, and the moment passed, but I still had the feeling he had been about to say something else.

"So tell me about your date," I said, and he spent the next few minutes filling me in on Jennifer, a graphic designer from Bountiful, a returned missionary from Ecuador (they had shared some of their conversation in Spanish), and an attractive, pleasant person.

"It sounds like you enjoyed her company," I concluded, and Noah agreed that he had.

"Maybe I will take her out again," he said, then added, "Speaking of company, you and Justin sure hit it off quickly."

I grinned. "Yeah, we did, didn't we? Did he say anything about me?"

"Just that he was looking forward to joining us again tomorrow."

"Hmm. That could mean he's just eager for more good food."

"You know that's not what he's interested in," Noah said, effectively turning the tables so that we were now talking about my love life instead of his. I asked him about his and Justin's time together in the mission field, and Noah told me they had been companions during one of the most difficult but productive periods of his mission, when they had both been released as zone leaders in other areas and then been brought together to open a small village where the gospel had never been taught before. They had shared some powerful conversion experiences, a fair number of baptisms, and some good times. "Justin is a faithful missionary and a great friend," Noah concluded. "I wouldn't mind at all if you two got something going."

I smiled. "I wouldn't mind that, either."

"Then I guess it's full speed ahead," he said. "Come on, let's get these dishes cleaned up."

As we worked together, I realized how much it had meant to me to have Justin work beside me in the kitchen the day before. Some of my most companionable moments with family members had happened in the kitchen during necessary but otherwise tedious work, and one of the things that had always bugged me about Kyle was the way he'd wait in the other room while I prepared meals or cleaned up after them. I decided at that moment to put this quality on my list of Necessary Attributes for a Potential Husband: The person I married someday had to be willing to work beside me in the kitchen.

Using the many-hands-make-light-work principle, we finished in no time. Noah hung around, shooting the breeze a while longer, but eventually he said he'd see me for my birthday dinner the next day at Mom and Dad's house, and he left.

I spent a little while just sitting by the window, thinking and saying a little prayer. I remembered the picture of the Lord's *Embrace,* and thanked Him for new opportunities. Perhaps the time had come when I could really put Kyle and my broken engagement behind me. Maybe Justin was the one who could help me move on. I picked up a knitting project I had started—a receiving blanket for Deb's new baby. It wasn't long before I caught myself humming a little tune, an old love song, the same tune Shari had been humming in the car the night before. I grinned at myself and hummed a little louder.

Chapter 5

That Saturday went splendidly, as well as I ever could have asked. By the time Shari and I drove back home that evening, I was pretty thoroughly twitterpated, and I had every reason to believe Justin was feeling the same way.

I had entered Mom's kitchen around noon to find not my usual carrot cake, but a chocolate layer cake with thick chocolate fudge frosting. When I asked where my carrot cake was, Mom said, "In the fridge." That's when Justin stepped into the kitchen to say, "The chocolate one is mine."

It turns out—and frankly, I'm still amazed by this—that Justin's birthday was the following day, November twenty-fifth, so he and I were sharing the family party. "I hope you don't mind," he said as he helped my mother cut vegetables for the salad. He looked so adorable, standing there in my family's kitchen. I'd have given him a kidney if he'd asked for it.

"Mind? You may have to fight me for it. I'll defend my birthday to the death." I gave him a pretend glare.

"This could be interesting," Justin said. "Do I get my choice of weapons?" He grinned, and I felt the thrill clean through to my toes.

We had curried turkey over brown rice and all the other trimmings I associated with my birthday celebration, and Justin seemed to be enjoying all of it as much as I was. Then there were two rounds of happy-birthday songs and greetings, two cakes to share, and more card games and TV football.

When it came time to open gifts, I realized I was unprepared. Justin had a gift for me, a pretty charm bracelet in sterling silver. The charms were thoughtful reminders of the time we'd already spent together and of other things he knew about me, including a broken-down jalopy suspended from the end of a tow truck, a tree house, a slice of pie, and a swing. I lifted it out of the box, and Justin fastened the clasp for me. That's when I realized I had no way to reciprocate.

Just as I opened my mouth to say so, Noah spoke up. "Hang on just a minute. Sarah's gift for you is in my room."

Over Justin's head, I gave my brother a panicked, deer-in-the-headlights look, but he mouthed, "Trust me" and headed for his bedroom. Moments later, he was back with a pretty package, neatly wrapped in silver foil paper with "Happy Birthday" written in the stripes. There was even a silver-and-white bow. The simple card read, "To Justin, from Sarah. Happy birthday." So far, so good. I held my breath while Justin carefully removed the wrapping.

Inside was a cardboard box, and inside the box was a framed picture of the two of us together at our Thanksgiving-night Rook game. The frame read "Birthday Memories" in raised letters, and the picture was flattering to both of us. We were clowning for the camera and looked like a pair of happy friends—or even a couple. Although I only vaguely remembered Noah shooting the picture, I smiled and said, "You're welcome" to Justin's thanks, mouthed a big "Thank you!" to Noah over Justin's head, and made a mental note that I owed my brother big-time. I was both surprised and pleased by Noah's good taste; "my" gift showed just the right level of personal interest without presuming anything. I couldn't have done better if I really had picked it myself.

Presents were followed by another Rook tournament in which Justin and I handily defeated all challengers. When we said good-bye at the door, he kissed my cheek and asked, "Can I call you this week?" Of course I said yes, hoping the stars in my eyes weren't too obvious. If I hadn't had Shari and Kerry with me, I think I could have saved some expensive gasoline by simply floating home.

The weeks following our mutual birthday could only be described as idyllic. My journal was full of Justin Owen. Despite end-of-term projects and finals and the drive up from Provo, he made the time to see me a couple of times each week. Each time we got to know each other a little better, and I even discovered he was a better kisser than Kyle.

We visited an exhibit at Thanksgiving Point, where Justin told me about growing up with three brothers and two sisters and I told him about my broken engagement. We went ice skating in downtown Salt Lake while he told me about playing behind the scenes at Disney World, where his dad still worked, and I told him about how I'd come to have my house. We went to a Christmas concert, then walked around in a nearby mall afterward, strolling hand-in-hand and window shopping as an excuse to spend more time together. He talked about playing high school sports and the disappointment of breaking his ankle at the start of basketball season his senior year. I told him about the disappointment of seeing Kyle's wedding announcement. As we drove around the new Daybreak Temple, he shared his doubts about accepting his mission call; I admitted I had felt doubts about accepting Kyle's proposal.

As Christmas drew near, I felt we were becoming close and even important to each other. Certainly I'd disclosed more about myself to Justin than I ever had to anyone—with the exception of you-know-who.

I approached the week before Christmas feeling about half in love and optimistic about the other half. When Deb teased me about getting a ring for Christmas, I laughed it off, but I called Jeanie to ask her opinion about quick relationships (she and her husband were engaged within three weeks of the day they met), and in my journal I secretly wondered if it might happen. Justin was certainly giving me all the right signals.

I began to ponder what I'd say if he did ask. We'd known each other such a short time, and yet everything seemed perfect, almost as if Justin was the answer I'd been praying for. But did I truly love him? Did I feel about him the way I had once felt about Kyle? Nagging at the back of my mind was the question of whether I had ever really loved Kyle, or whether it was just my pride and not my heart that had been broken by his betrayal. When Justin called me three days before Christmas and asked if he could come to see me that evening so we could "just talk for awhile," I began to consider a possible answer to his possible question.

It was the last day of school before the holiday break, and my third graders were as squirrely as I'd ever seen them. I had to keep reminding myself that these were unusual circumstances requiring extraordinary patience. Thank goodness the Brenner girls had reached an armed truce; had I had their war to deal with in addition to the sugar-fueled adrenaline high of the rest of my class, I think I'd have gone home with a headache before the day was half over.

As it was, I had ordered two rambunctious boys down off desks, stopped a paper-plane dogfight by catching one of the miscreant objects in midair, and said, "Shh! Quiet down!" at least fifty times before the final bell rang and the children spilled out of my thoroughly trashed classroom. That's not to mention taking Henry Jackson, usually one of my models of ideal behavior, to the office for spitting—spitting!—on the boy beside him in the lunch line. No one was happier than I was to see the end of that day.

I might even have cancelled with Justin if he hadn't made the evening sound so important. As it was, I scooted home and took a long, soothing bath, put on some comfy (but cute!) loungers and some soft, romantic music, and brewed a pot of spiced apple cider. Then I sipped a cup and doodled in the margins of my journal as I waited—wanting to write something but uncertain what to say, and thankful that Shari and her daughter had made other plans. I had relaxed just enough to begin to doze when Justin rang my doorbell.

I invited him in and took his coat as he entered. He looked so bleak that I wondered if his day had been as bad as mine, so I asked.

"Not really," he answered, but he wouldn't meet my eyes. A tingle of foreboding ran down my spine.

"Come in. Sit down," I offered, and Justin sat. "Would you like a cup of cider?"

"No thank you, Sarah. Please. Come sit. There's something I've got to say."

Even as I sat, I knew I wasn't going to like what came next, but I was completely unprepared for the words that followed.

"I'm sorry, Sarah, but I don't think we should see each other anymore."

I smiled. This had to be a joke, right? A moment ago I'd been thinking he might propose. "You're not serious . . ." I began.

"I'm afraid it just isn't working," he said, finally looking at me, and I could see that he *was* serious. Deadly so.

I couldn't think of a response. Part of me wanted to save face. Another part wanted to scream and cry and throw a raging tantrum, sure this couldn't be happening *again*. A third part wanted answers, and that part won. "Why not?" I asked, trying to keep wounded pride out of my voice. "I thought things were going well."

"I guess it depends on how you define well," he said. "Face it, Sarah. You're still involved with your ex."

"That's ridiculous!" I shouted. Was he serious? A wild stampede couldn't have dragged me back to Kyle—even if he wasn't a married man. "You can't mean what you're saying! There's nothing between Kyle and me. I haven't even seen him in months. He's married to someone else, for Pete's sake!"

"And you haven't gotten over that, have you?"

"That's ridicu—" I began again, but Justin cut me off.

"I didn't say you were in love with him, Sarah. I said you were still *involved* with him—and emotionally, you are. So involved in fact that you can't talk or think about anything else."

"That's ridi—"

"Think about it. What have you talked about every time we've been together this month?"

I opened my mouth to answer him and, to my ultimate horror, realized he was right. My mind went blank as the pictures flashed before my eyes. But I didn't have to speak. Justin was on a roll.

"When we walked at Thanksgiving Point, you talked about your ex. When we went ice skating, you talked about your ex. When we got ice cream after the concert, you talked about your ex. Even when we drove around the temple, you couldn't talk about anything but your ex. Since we began dating, you've hardly talked about anything else."

"I . . . I thought we were getting to know each other," I answered, but it sounded lame even to me. To my shame, my eyes were filling with tears. "I thought I was sharing important things from my background with someone I cared about."

"In a way that's my point," Justin said. When I looked in his eyes, I saw pity—which made me feel even worse. "The most important thing in your background, the one thing you most want to share, is how you feel about Kyle and how Kyle hurt you and all the anger you feel toward Kyle. I kept hoping you'd move on, but you didn't. I'm sorry, Sarah, but if you don't learn to forgive, you're going to poison any relationship."

I jumped to my feet, hot anger flooding through me. "How dare you!" I shrieked. "You have no right to judge me!"

To my surprise, he stood too, and readily agreed. "You're right. I have no right. But I think other guys will feel the same way if you keep throwing Kyle at them the way you did at me, or if all you ever talk about is your broken heart."

I gasped and tried to form a retort, but couldn't think of a single response. I stood there stunned and stinging while Justin walked across my small living room, took his coat from my closet, and opened the front door. "I'm sorry, Sarah," he said. "I hope it all works out for you someday." Then he walked out of my door and out of my life.

I must have stood there, mouth hanging open, for a good two minutes before I sank into my chair. What I wanted more than anything was to throw a raging, sobbing pity party, but the sobs wouldn't come.

Maybe I was still too much in shock. I know I sat there a long, long time in absolute silence, quiet tears forming a steady trickle while I absorbed Justin's last words. As much as I wanted to scream and argue, I couldn't. He was right. Hadn't the Spirit tried to teach me that same lesson weeks earlier? Maybe things could have been different if I had listened then. Despite my shock and hurt pride, two things were absolutely clear: There was no future for Justin and me, and I had some serious spiritual work to do. It was time I began my quest for understanding and forgiveness, whether I liked it or not.

I tried to write in my journal but couldn't make the words form on the page. When I finally did write, the ink was smeared with tears. Sometime after ten, I took the cider off the stove and turned off the burner, washed my face, and knelt to say my prayers. It was more difficult to conjure the image of a smiling, approving Savior. I said a simple prayer asking His forgiveness and pleading for His help instead.

It was a while before I dozed off, but I was still awake enough to hear Shari come in. Someone else was with her, and there was some whispering while they put Kerry to bed and said good night. Then I heard Shari humming quiet Christmas carols as she brushed her teeth and readied herself for sleep. Before I fell asleep, I thought how glad I was that her evening had gone so much better than mine.

Chapter 6

Epiphany: e·piph·a·ny \i-ˈpi-fə-nē\
n. pl. e·piph·a·nies

1. A sudden manifestation of the essence or meaning
of something.

2. A comprehension or perception of reality by means
of a sudden intuitive realization: "I experienced an
epiphany, a spiritual flash that would change the way I
viewed myself" (Frank Maier).

3. A moment of startling insight.

4. Proper noun: The Christian celebration that culmi-
nates the season of Advent and Christmas, usually
celebrated January sixth.

Epiphany. I'd known the word since Mrs. McPherson assigned it
for vocab-spelling in eighth-grade English, but I'd rarely experienced
real epiphanies, at least not in such cycling spirals as I did during that
Christmas season. The first came with Justin that evening the week
before Christmas, and the second came when the Spirit confirmed the
truth of his words. The third was during our Christmas Eve celebration at my parents' home.

It was a typical Kimball gathering with noise and food and children darting in and out as the grown-ups tried to visit. Shari and

Kerry had gone to spend the holiday with an aunt nearby, and, of course, Justin wouldn't have come even if he hadn't gone to Florida, so it was just family. Dinner was the usual Christmas potluck with all our favorite dishes—I brought the ambrosia fruit salad and stuffed celery—followed by our annual Christmas Eve program. Dad read the story from Luke, and Mom read the story from 3 Nephi about a day, a night, and a day without darkness. Then the grandchildren, with Brittan directing, presented their own little Christmas pageant.

Eight-year-old Emily, Josh and Barbara's eldest, played Mary. She wore her mom's bathrobe and a towel on her head, but she kept a reverent expression as she rode on the back of the donkey, convincingly portrayed by Deb's son, Ryan. Her brother Dylan played Joseph, and a bevy of adorable toddlers in towels became the adoring shepherds. Timmy even carried a staff—a scrub oak branch his father had cut and stripped for him. The only awkward moment came when Mary started to lose her balance and the donkey reached up to steady her. Though we all chuckled and thanked the donkey, there was a warm spirit among us as we watched the next generation re-create the tale of Christ's birth in a stable. When Emily laid her doll in a cardboard box filled with crumpled newspaper, I actually choked up a bit—and I wasn't the only one.

The brief pageant ended, and we got out the pipe chimes Mom had made one year in Relief Society and played the same carols we always play. I had the number-six chime, so I played very little in most songs but really had to pay attention during "Jingle Bells." The sibling gift exchange followed. Tim and Josh gave each other joke ties, and Deb gave Noah a gorgeous hand-knit sweater. She must have worked on it every day since Thanksgiving. It was shaped and cabled and absolutely beautiful, and Noah put it on immediately. Seth and his wife seemed delighted with the DVDs I had given their family, and I tried not to look dismayed when I realized Ruth had drawn my name, since I was fairly certain what I'd find in her prettily wrapped package. I even managed to smile as I thanked her for my new membership in Mormons2Marry.com.

"You have to register to get it started," Ruthie cautioned, obviously eager to get me going.

"I'll get right to that," I said, trying to keep my expression pleasant.

"I could help you with it before you go," she offered.

I rushed to cut her off. "Not tonight, Ruth."

"But—"

"I will register soon, though. Thanks."

Ruth might have pressed if Dad hadn't announced that dessert was ready. We finished the evening with Mom's homemade eggnog and apple pie, then gathered around the TV like we always do to watch *It's a Wonderful Life.*

The credits were just beginning when Elise crawled into my lap and we cuddled up under her favorite blankie. It was then that my next epiphany arrived. Just before young George Bailey dived into the icy water to save his brother, just as Elise was drifting away, she said, "I hope Santa brings you something really good, Auntie Sarah. Then maybe you won't have to be so angry and sad all the time." She snuggled against me and sagged peacefully into sleep while I sat there stroking her hair and choking on a lump of pain and guilt so thick I thought it might strangle me. Until that moment I hadn't realized how openly I had worn my personal heartbreak or that it had caused so much hurt and worry for the wonderful people I loved, even the little ones. I resolved to make a major change as "learning forgiveness" jumped to the number-one spot on my list of New Year's resolutions.

That moment of personal crisis aside, the feeling in the room with my family was so warm and sweet that I might have stayed if I hadn't promised to feed Harry. It was just as well that I didn't stay, since Deb and Brian and their whole brood were over-nighting to give my seriously pregnant sister a break from some of the Christmas hassle. Still, my own small home felt drearily empty after the family crowd scene, and I have to admit I brooded a bit, wondering again if I was destined to spend my life alone.

I spent a long time cuddling Harry, who tolerated it even though he stopped purring within the first half minute. As I sat there, I suddenly had an image of myself inserted into an old movie I'd once seen about two elderly spinsters who lived together and spent their evenings rocking in their living room and stroking their tabby cats. I couldn't see the face of the woman who rocked beside me, but I couldn't imagine it being cute, vivacious Shari, who had so much going for her. Still, the image of me with my silver hair in a bun was crystal clear, and it wasn't pretty.

I stood up rather abruptly, dumping a disgruntled Harry onto the floor, and marched myself off to record my day in my journal and prepare myself for bed. Before I said my prayers, I spent a while on my knees, trying to call up the image of that lovely painting again. My prayers were more poignant than ever as I asked the Lord to bless me with a change of heart, to give me charity and forgiveness toward those who had caused me pain, and to help me let go of old injuries. It was the most agonizing Christmas Eve I'd ever spent—a kind of small, personal Gethsemane that made me even more thankful for the birth of my Savior and the gift of His Atonement.

It was in that moment, in the last instant of consciousness before sleep as I pondered the Lord's sacrifice, that I experienced my next great epiphany: If our Savior had atoned for my shortcomings, hadn't He also atoned for Kyle's? Even for the covenants that Kyle had broken with Him, more serious than the breaking of any promises he had made to me. And if the Savior could forgive him, in fact had already forgiven him, what on earth was my problem?

The insight came in a flash, passing through me like a shock and taking with it a large measure of the bitterness that had left such a foul taste in my mouth during recent months, easing some of the pain from my heart. As sleep overcame me, I knew my spiritual heavy lifting had just begun, but it was a strong beginning. I was already letting go of much of the anger I had nurtured so well for so long.

* * *

Christmas dawned bright and beautiful—crisp and clear and startlingly white due to a light snowfall in the early morning hours. I puttered around the house for a couple of hours, feeding Harry and enjoying the morning paper with a cup of hot chocolate before putting on my pink sweater and a pair of dark slacks and heading across the valley to Mom and Dad's. I wanted to give Deb and Brian a little time to enjoy the morning with their kids and the grandparents before I intruded. As I drove over the Jordan River and up the other side of the valley, I sang carols, promising myself I would put on a happier face than my family had seen from me lately.

"G'morning, Auntie Sarah!" three-year-old Nolan, Deb's youngest, said and ran up and threw his arms around me just above the knees, hugging me with such fierce energy that I had to steady myself against the doorjamb. It was just the start I needed to banish the last of my selfish blue funk. The rest of the gang welcomed me just as warmly, and I enjoyed watching Deb and Brian's little ones playing with their family gifts. We ate Mom's homemade cinnamon rolls with apple cider and eggnog while the Tabernacle Choir's Christmas album played in the background on Dad's new CD player and the older kids indulged five-year-old Maren in yet another game of Chutes and Ladders.

It was in the midst of the late-morning quiet that my next epiphany came. Deb, her due date less than two weeks away now, went into one of the back bedrooms to lie down for awhile, and Brian took the kids out to build a snowman in the front yard. I was loading the dishwasher when Noah came up behind me and put his hand on my shoulder. "Hey, sis. When you're finished here, do you have a minute?"

"Yeah, sure. In fact," I closed the dishwasher, "I'm finished now. What's up?"

"Just come with me," he said, so I dried my hands and followed Noah down the hall to his old bedroom, the one he still used whenever he visited. I stepped inside and Noah went to his closet. "There's one more gift for you," he said and produced a small, pretty package.

"Noah, you shouldn't have—" I began.

"I didn't," he interrupted. "Go ahead and open it. I'll give you a minute alone." He stepped into the hall, closing the door behind him.

I didn't know what to think. If it wasn't from Noah, then who? Suddenly my knees went weak, and I sank down on the end of Noah's bed. I looked for a card, but there wasn't one, not even under the pretty silver bow. But that bow looked awfully familiar. Fortifying my courage with a deep breath, I began unwrapping. It was a book, President Kimball's *The Miracle of Forgiveness*, and there was a hand-written inscription inside the front cover:

Dear Sarah,

I hope you are having a wonderful holiday. I have
thought of you often, hoping there are no hard feelings between us. I hope you can forgive any hurt I
caused you. You are a wonderful woman, and you
deserve only the best.

Fondly,
Justin

I suppose the tears were predictable. Even the nature of Justin's
gift was predictable, given all that had passed between us. What I
hadn't predicted was that there'd be a gift at all. The fact that there
was, and that so much thought and concern had gone into it, helped
me realize that Justin had cared. That realization warmed and reassured me.

Although I knew there wasn't time at that moment to get into the
deep doctrine of President Kimball's book, I turned to the first
chapter and began to read, telling myself I just wanted a little taste.
What I got was so much more than that, for as I read through the
first few pages, I was struck with a new and blinding epiphany—
something that should have been obvious from the start: *Kyle didn't
need* my *forgiveness*. He had moved on with his life and probably
rarely even thought about me. *I* was the one who needed the forgiveness. I needed to forgive Kyle in order to heal my own life, just as
Justin had said. Even more important, I needed the Lord's forgiveness
for harboring such a stubborn and unforgiving heart.

By then I was sobbing. I slid to my knees and prayed again,
repeating the experience of the night before, only this time with a
heart full of gratitude. Somewhere in the midst of my prayer, I heard
the door open and quietly close again, and I was distantly aware that
someone had looked in to check on me, but for some time I just
stayed there on my knees, letting the gratitude flow out while the
realizations sank in, one after another, as I came a little closer to
understanding what my Savior's Atonement meant to me. It was one
of the most tender, most cleansing hours I had ever spent, and I spent
it all on my knees.

I enjoyed that Christmas Day more than I'd enjoyed anything in months. My spirit was lighter, my thoughts happier than they'd been for nearly a year. In the middle of an impromptu snowball fight with my nephews and nieces, I realized I was laughing—not the forced, appropriate kind of laugh I'd been adopting since the Kyle fiasco, but real, happy laughter.

My family noticed the difference. When we came inside to warm up with a stoked fireplace and hot chocolate, Brittan asked if maybe I was feeling better, and I half crushed her against me as I answered with a heartfelt, "Yes!" Even my missionary brother, Mark, noticed it during our hour-long family phone call to Texas. Mom told me that he had commented to her about my "new upbeat attitude" after I said good-bye and handed the extension phone to Noah. Later I called Jeanie in Denver to wish her and her husband a merry Christmas, and practically the first thing she said was, "Something must have happened, Sarah. You sound so much better." And I *was* better. I knew it.

That Christmas epiphany was the beginning of real healing. During the week between Christmas and New Year's, I took one full day at the school to put up bulletin boards and to prep for the coming week—curriculum materials, handouts, lesson plans, and the like. I also took some time to pen a short, careful, and heartfelt thank-you to Justin, telling him what his gift had meant to me. Except for those few hours, and another few spent catching up with Shari and Kerry between their visits to various relatives, I spent most of that week reading *The Miracle of Forgiveness* and the scriptures it referenced, writing each new discovery in my journal.

I'd heard others joke after reading President Kimball's book that the miracle is that anyone is ever forgiven. I didn't feel that way at all. Maybe it was the spiritual preparation I had already made, but I read each page with gratitude, amazement at the Savior's love, and joy that a process had been established to help me to clear old wounds from my heart and be made whole again. I practically devoured the book, and when I finished it for the first time, I sat down and read it again.

It was during that second reading that the next epiphany came, and it was so clear and obvious that I was embarrassed that I hadn't seen it sooner. It came as I was reading Isaiah's prophecies concerning the Lord's Atonement, specifically in the words, "Surely he hath borne our griefs, and carried our sorrows."

The first thing that struck me was the past tense: He *hath* borne our griefs. Of course I knew that Christ's Atonement had already happened, but it wasn't until that moment that I took the scripture to heart, likening it to my own life as the prophet Nephi had counseled. I wiped at a tear and read Isaiah's words again. "Surely he hath borne *my* griefs . . ." And the Spirit confirmed it was so. Then, just as I began to absorb that concept, two other words jumped out at me: *griefs* and *sorrows*. Not sins, but sorrows. And that was my next great epiphany. I realized that Christ's Atonement wasn't just good for forgiveness, but for solace and comfort as well.

Somehow, in an infinite sacrifice that my finite mind could not grasp, the Savior had already suffered for my heartbreak and wounded pride, my indignation and pain. I didn't need to feel all that anger and angst about what had happened with Kyle, because my Redeemer had already drunk of that bitter cup in my behalf. The relief that swept over me was the most genuine, most freeing sensation I had ever felt—*ever*. I couldn't say I was fully over my selfishness or my hurt feelings, but I knew I had passed an important milestone and that the anguish of the past would never again have the same power to intrude on my present—or my future.

It seemed more than coincidence when my January *Ensign* arrived that week and the inside cover had a painting that looked vaguely familiar. Though it wasn't *Embrace*—I'd have known that painting anywhere—it had the same impressionistic background and photographic human qualities I recognized. This painting showed the Savior overlooking the temple in Jerusalem, a small child at His knee. It was titled, *And a Little Child Shall Lead Them*. I noticed the artist's name, Craig Emory, and though I couldn't say I remembered it, I knew he must have been the one whose painting had been in the MFA exhibit that had meant so much to me. I said a quick, silent prayer thanking God for artists like Brother Emory, whose talent could help others aspire to reach toward heaven.

* * *

On New Year's Eve, I joined the family for dinner and played board games with family stragglers rather than going out on the town alone. Although I'd often enjoyed Salt Lake's First Night celebration, this didn't seem the time for it. The family invited me to come back the next day, but I skipped their impromptu New Year's Day gathering in order to be at home when Shari got back from her family visits.

Shari arrived in the early evening with an exhausted Kerry already sleeping in her car seat. I helped Shari put her daughter to bed, and then she and I sipped some cocoa and caught up on recent events. As the evening got later and Harry crawled, purring, into Shari's lap, I was struck by the memory of the spinster movie and wondered if I should maybe buy us a couple of rocking chairs, but this time the thought came with gentle humor. As I shared my recent epiphanies with Shari, I found that most of my bitterness was already gone.

"So does that mean you're ready to meet someone new?" Shari asked, settling in as if for a long story.

"I don't know," I answered, trying to be honest even with myself. "Justin was right about how involved I've been with my own hurt emotions. I thought I was ready awhile ago, but it seems I really wasn't. How about you? Are you over what happened to you and Kerry? That was clearly worse than anything that happened to me."

"Who can tell what was worse?" Shari said. "If it hurts, it hurts. Right?"

"Maybe so," I answered, "but the point is, are *you* ready to meet someone new?"

"Mmm." Shari looked away, not quite meeting my eyes.

"Shari! You've already met someone, haven't you?" I pulled my knees up under my chin and leaned forward, eager to hear it all. "Haven't you?" I pressed.

"Maybe," she answered, her eyes crinkling at the corners.

"So come on, then. Tell Auntie Sarah all about it."

Shari grinned. "You're not *my* Auntie Sarah!" With that, my ailing mantel clock struck a discordant eleven chimes, and Shari announced it was time for bed.

"No fair!" I grumbled and followed her into the kitchen, but my efforts to persuade her to spill the beans were without effect as she rinsed her cocoa cup and put it in the sink, then trotted down the hall and disappeared into the room she shared with her daughter.

I went to sleep that evening knowing I was ready to face the new work week and the New Year, grateful for a season full of Christmas and Christ and some of the greatest spiritual growth I had ever experienced. My image of the Savior's *Embrace* danced in my thoughts as I drifted into rest.

Chapter 7

That second day of January, school began with such noise and buzz and confusion that I feared we were looking at another day like the last one before vacation. While I wanted to settle down to the lessons and materials I had prepared the week before, the kids all wanted to talk about where they went and who they saw and what they got for Christmas. After trying to fight that trend for several minutes, I decided to go with it.

I started in one corner and went around the room, giving all the kids who wanted to a couple of minutes to tell us what they did for Christmas and what their favorite gift was. To my surprise, it worked. No one took unfair advantage or insisted on reeling off long lists of everything Santa had left under the tree. By the time we'd finished the circuit, the kids were focused and ready to work. I made a mental note to remember that trick for future holidays.

The rest of the day went swimmingly. Henry Jackson got one hundred percent on his math review—for the first time ever—and the whole class helped him celebrate his achievement with applause and congratulations. Veronica de Guzman gave her oral book report—her first in English—and the class was just as eager in offering her their support. Even the Brenner twins were on their best behavior. Just before the final bell, Ellen confided that one of her goals for the coming year was to help her sister get a perfect score on every spelling test. I congratulated her on a very worthwhile goal. When the final bell found the whole class neatly in line and ready to go, I was feeling fairly successful. I went home that evening feeling grateful and reflecting on the fact that gratitude seemed to have become a major theme in my life over the past couple of weeks.

An hour later, I reminded myself about the importance of gratitude as I cleaned up a laundry room full of filthy water and suds, the result of a major malfunction in my ancient washing machine. When I was finished, I immediately went to the telephone and called my dear, patient brother Noah.

"Your washing machine? What's wrong with it?" he asked.

"It's like the lilies of the field," I answered, biting my lip. "It toils not. Neither doth it spin."

"I'll be right there," he answered, and he arrived within thirty minutes. Within just a few more minutes, he had pronounced my old machine dead, or at least needing repairs too expensive to make them worthwhile, since I probably needed a new machine anyway. By then Shari had joined us in the laundry area; she had arrived home just in time to hear Noah's diagnosis. I saw her face fall and realized that what would be a major inconvenience for me came closer to being a disaster for Shari. With the thin margins in her monthly budget, the cost of a laundromat could possibly mean giving up food. I took a deep breath and then took a plunge.

"I'd been planning to get a new machine after the first of the year anyway," I lied smoothly, knowing I'd have to put it on credit and pay for it piecemeal. I was pretty sure I'd seen an offer for six months with no interest . . .

"Really, Sarah? I'd hate to have you run up a debt for a washing machine."

"Don't worry about it. I'll probably need a few days to find the right machine and arrange for its delivery, but if you don't mind taking your laundry out maybe once or twice, I should have a new machine in here by this time next week."

Shari looked so relieved I wanted to cry. "I'm sure that will be fine," she said. Then she gave me such a searching look it made me feel guilty for my little white lie. "You're sure about this?"

"Absolutely!" I assured her. "In fact, I think I'll go washing machine shopping right after dinner."

"My week to cook," Shari said. "I'll get started right away."

"Tell you what," Noah cut in. "Let's all go out for pizza. My treat."

"Yay!" We all looked at Kerry, who had thrown both hands in the air.

Noah said, "I guess that settles it."

"Yes, I guess it does," Shari said, and started helping her grinning two-year-old back into her coat.

"I want papperini!" Kerry announced, and Noah laughed.

"Then I guess it will be one-half papperini and one-half combination," Noah said, and I wondered if he knew that Shari loved combination pizza. "Does that work for everybody?"

We all agreed, then Noah turned to me. "Sis, if you want to drive your own car so you can go shopping after, I'll be happy to give these ladies a ride home."

"Sounds good." I grabbed my coat and got my purse, but what with trying to find Kerry's shoes again and looking for my keys, it took us a long time before we finally got out the door.

We planned to meet up at our favorite local pizza place a few minutes later. I arrived first and placed our order, then found a table and sat around wondering what was keeping the others. Noah and Shari arrived just before the food was ready, and Noah made good on his offer to pay for everybody's dinner.

The family-sized pizza was huge, and we stuffed ourselves on all the pizza we could hold. When we were finished, Kerry insisted on riding the "horsie ride," and Noah spent a couple more bucks in quarters while Kerry went around and around and *around* in circles. Noah finally convinced Kerry that he was out of quarters, and they came back to the table. We were all putting our coats on, getting ready to go back into the January chill, when Noah's cell phone rang.

I went on helping Kerry into her jacket, not paying attention to Noah's phone call until I heard him gasp, "Oh, no!" I looked around just in time to see him drop to the bench. His face had gone starkly white. "Okay," he said. "We'll be right there." Then he turned to me. "That was Mom. Deb is hemorrhaging. They've rushed her to the hospital."

"No!" I felt the color drain from my face as well, and I sank down beside Noah.

"You two go ahead," Shari said. "If you leave in Noah's car, you can go straight over without having to worry about taking us home. That is, if you don't mind me taking your car, Sarah."

"Huh?" I had heard all the words, but my shell-shocked mind hadn't made any sense of them.

Noah stood. "Come on, Sarah. We'll take my car to the hospital. Shari and Kerry can go home in yours. I'll see that you get home later."

"Oh. Yes. Right," I answered and got into my coat. Shari had to reach into my purse to fetch my keys.

I can't tell you much about that next couple of hours. Noah and I arrived to find half the family there and the other half on the way, along with a large group of Myersons, Brian's family. It was a little after eight, Deb was in surgery, and nobody knew what to expect. We gathered all the Kimballs and Myersons in a corner of the waiting room for a kneeling family prayer in behalf of Deborah and her baby. After that we all sort of milled about, trying to offer what comfort we could to Brian, who was somewhere between frantic and desolate. I kept trying to picture our loving Savior with His arms open, but I had to cut the image off. If I imagined Him opening His arms to receive my sister, there was too much unintended meaning.

A little after nine, a nurse came out to tell us that Deb and Brian's daughter had been successfully delivered by C-section and seemed to be doing well. At nearly full term, she weighed just under nine pounds and was twenty inches long. We were all thrilled to know the baby was well, yet our worry for Deb overshadowed the announcement.

The next ninety minutes crept by as we took turns pacing and sitting, comforting and pacing. Every time the door opened, we all held our breath, but no one had any real news yet, just that the doctors were doing what they could and that Deb was "holding her own"—a medical euphemism I took to mean my sister was still alive. It was nearly eleven before Deb's obstetrical surgeon, Dr. Keegan, came out. As a group we stood to meet him, but it was Brian the surgeon looked for. We cleared a path, then circled the two men as they met in the middle of the waiting room.

I may never forget the doctor's first words: "Your wife gave us quite a scare, but it looks like she's going to make it."

"Thank God." Brian nearly staggered from relief while the rest of the family began to breathe again.

The next part was something of a blur as well as we all tried to follow Dr. Keegan's explanation amid our tears and sniffles. I caught phrases like "probably began simply" and "quietly bleeding out" and "lost a lot of blood," but I was mostly listening for his assessment of how Deb would do from this point on. When I heard, "Assuming a normal recovery, she should be able to go home within the next five or six days," my brain finally kicked in again.

"Can I see her?" Brian asked. Some color was coming back into his face.

"She'll be in recovery for another hour or so," Dr. Keegan answered. "You'll be allowed to see her as soon as the nurses are ready to wheel her up to her room."

"She'll want to see the baby as soon as possible," Brian said. "Is it okay with you if I carry her over to meet Deb when she comes out of recovery?"

"It's okay with me. Just make sure to check with the nursery staff," he answered.

We all thanked Dr. Keegan profusely, then we family members helped each other piece together and make sense of his explanation, and this time I got most of it.

Apparently Deb had begun a sluggish labor sometime during the early morning hours, but her labor had dragged on slowly throughout the day. Since this was her fifth pregnancy, Deb had expected everything to move faster this time, not slower, and had finally insisted on going to the hospital. Brian had found a neighbor to keep an eye on the kids, and they had been on their way to the hospital when the hemorrhaging had begun. Then Brian, in a panic, had driven the last five blocks to Alta View at nearly seventy miles per hour, hitting his horn to clear intersections.

According to the doctor, "uterine atony," a lack of muscle tone or the failure of the uterus to contract adequately, had resulted in tearing, and as one problem led to another, Deb's whole body had begun shutting down. It had taken multiple transfusions, great surgical skill, and probably a few miracles to save her. When Brian asked what caused uterine atony, the doctor told him that it just happened sometimes and was more common among older mothers who had already had multiple deliveries.

"Deb wasn't sure if she wanted to quit at five," Brian concluded as he summed up his wife's condition for the rest of us, "but I'm thinking five is a really nice number."

Mom looked slightly embarrassed. "That will be up to the two of you to decide, dear."

"I'm afraid not," Brian corrected. "Part of saving her was an emergency hysterectomy. We have our full family now." There was an awkward pause as we all absorbed that, and then Brian looked up at the clock. "Whoa! Deb will be waking up soon. I'd better go see Dr. Wiser about bringing the baby down."

"Can we see her, too?" It was Ruth, who had hitched a ride with Josh and Barbara.

"Not tonight," Brian answered. "We're way past visiting hours now. They're only letting me in because Dr. Keegan okayed it—and because they know they can't keep me out." He forced a slight smile. "Come back tomorrow morning, and I'm sure she'll be thrilled to see all of you."

We all hugged Brian and told him to send our best wishes and prayers to Deb. Then he left to get his new baby, and we all started toward the parking lot.

"Does anyone know if they have a name yet?" I asked.

It was Dad who answered. "Last I heard, they had narrowed it to two possibilities, though they weren't yet ready to say what those were. I imagine they'll tell us tomorrow."

"That sounds good." I tried not to sound disappointed, but I knew I wouldn't be able to be there in the morning when the others came to visit Deb and the baby. I wouldn't have missed being there with the family that night, but now that the crisis had passed, my duty to my third graders superseded my need to visit.

I finally got to see the baby after finishing my class the next day. Deb and Brian had decided to name her Lauren Caprice Myerson. Whatever they called her, it was easy for anyone to see that Lauren was going to be another beauty. Even at just one day old, she already had picture-perfect features and a creamy, flawless complexion. Deb assured me her daughter's good looks were due to her quick removal via C-section, zipper-style. "She's pretty," Deb explained, "because she didn't have to go through the trauma of ordinary birth." I knew better. Just like her mama, our Lauren would have been pretty no matter what trauma she'd been through.

That first afternoon I took Deb the knitted pink-and-white receiving blanket I had been struggling like mad to finish and which I'd put the final touches on during my lunch break at school that day. The hospital room was already full of flowers and gifts, not just from the family but from Deb and Brian's ward and neighbors and friends. It was clear that Lauren, like the rest of their family, was going to be dearly loved.

* * *

The next couple of days were a proverbial whirlwind as I tried to keep up the positive new beginning with my third graders, visit Deb and Lauren at least daily, and occasionally spell off Mom and the sisters from the Granite Stake who were holding down the fort for Brian and Deb while she remained hospitalized. Suddenly, I found myself at the end of the week with little clean clothing in my closet and chest of drawers; it was then that I remembered my promise to buy a new washer.

I did some looking that Friday evening but ended up hauling out several baskets and bags full of laundry on Saturday. Ironically it was on January sixth, the day when much of the Christian world celebrates Epiphany, that my next great epiphany struck, just when I was fairly certain there weren't any more to be had—at least, not on that same old subject.

I had just finished loading my wash into all the machines down a full lineup of washers when a young woman wheeled in a cart full of dirty laundry and looked in dismay at the bank of busy machines just starting their cycle. I pointed out the empty washers on the opposite side, and she seemed relieved.

She had an infant in a kangaroo pack curled up against her chest, and the effort of leaning over the sleeping baby to load the machines was clearly taxing. She looked so childlike and so strained, as if she were carrying way too much for someone as young and as small as she. There were dark shadows under her eyes, and my heart went out to her almost instantly. The strain of the burdens she carried showed in her face and in the way she straightened, bowing her back, with her hands pressed into the bend. Thinking immediately of Deb and her new baby, I jumped up.

"Let me help," I offered, coming around the machines.

"Oh, no, I couldn't intrude—"

"Nonsense. I don't have a thing to do while I wait for my wash, and it's obvious you're carrying plenty as it is." I pointed to the sleeping child. "At least let me help you load."

She smiled. "I'd be grateful."

We began a mini assembly line, with me lifting and her sorting the wash into various machines. To overcome any awkwardness she might still feel about the situation, I struck up a conversation. As I handed up a half dozen nice men's work shirts, I asked, "Have you been married long?"

"Not long," she said. "We were married last spring."

I couldn't help my quick look at the baby. Embarrassed at myself, I looked away and searched for something to say. "Spring is a nice time for a wedding."

"You're right in what you're thinking," she said with a sheepish smile. "We didn't wait for the wedding. It was one of many mistakes we made, but we're trying to put things right now." She paused, then asked somewhat tentatively, "Are you LDS?"

"Yes," I answered. "You, too?"

"Yeah. Actually it was my husband who taught and baptized me, back when we were in high school. He was a senior and I was just a freshman, and I think I would have done most anything to get his attention. I didn't take the Church as seriously then as I should have, and I was pretty annoyed when he decided to go on a mission rather than stay to marry me." I hope I didn't look disapproving, but she must have seen something in my face because she added, "Oh, don't misunderstand. He was worthy to go."

"Not my place to judge," I said, with what I hoped was a gentle smile, and handed her several pairs of men's dress slacks.

"We were both worthy then," she added quietly, almost to herself. Then she looked up at me again.

"When he got home, I was waiting for him, but his parents had arranged for him to enroll at BYU, and he came out here within days after he got off the plane. I hardly saw him at all."

"You said he came out here. Out here from where?" I asked, handing up some obviously used baby clothing, probably someone's hand-me-downs that had been through a few babies before coming to her.

"The Midwest," she said, and I felt my stomach lurch. This story was beginning to sound very familiar.

"Oh," I said over the lump in my throat, trying to sound like a disinterested party, although my interest had suddenly grown highly personal and very intense. "Really?"

"Yeah. He came out here and started dating other people. By the time he came home at Christmas, he already had plans to marry some other girl, somebody he knew from school in Provo."

I couldn't think of anything to say, so instead of speaking, I handed her another batch of baby clothes.

"I didn't know that then, of course. When he came home, I went to see him, and we took up almost immediately right where we'd left off, and then, well . . ." She paused, and a light blush warmed her pretty cheeks. "Things just kind of got away from us."

I nodded, my throat too tight for speech. It wasn't until she looked down at my empty hands that I remembered to hand up the last batch of baby clothes.

"By the time I realized I was pregnant, he'd already come back out here for the spring semester. I called him up to tell him the news, and that's when he told me he was getting married."

"What—" I cleared my throat. "What did you say?"

"I told him I didn't care who she was or what kind of claim she had on him. I needed him worse than she did, and he owed me and my baby." She started the last load and leaned back against the washer, resting her back. "I guess that was kinda mean, but I was feeling pretty desperate about then."

"Yes," I said. "Yes, I can imagine." Oddly, I found that I could.

"That's when I told Kyle, 'You'd better come back here and marry me, or I'm gonna get my daddy after you.' I guess that scared him. He broke it off with the other girl, left school, and came home. We got married a couple of weeks later."

By that time I was leaning heavily on the washer, feeling too weak to stand. Fearing I already knew the answer, I asked, "Kyle? Is your husband's name Kyle?"

She gave me a funny look. "Lyle," she said. "Lyle Adams. You know him?"

The whirring in my brain stopped instantly, but it took me a long moment to say, "No, I don't think I do."

The girl looked concerned. "Say, is something wrong? You're not crying, are you?"

"No! Uh, no," I answered, looking away. "I must just have . . . uh, laundry soap in my eye or something. I'm going to go wash it out."

By the time I returned, I had regained my composure, and the baby had started fussing. I took a few moments to admire the little one—a girl, as it turned out—and then the young mother, whose name was Lydia (not Beth) Adams (not Lewis), sat down to nurse her baby. Soon she started telling me about how she and her husband, Lyle, were working to make things right. "We plan to go to the temple next year if the bishop thinks we're ready," she told me. "I know what the Church means to me now—now that I almost lost it."

"That's great," I said. "About the temple, I mean. Congratulations." And I knew I actually meant it. As Lydia continued, I learned she was from Iowa, not Missouri, and that she hoped to be sealed in Nauvoo. When our wash loads were finished and dried and we prepared to go our separate ways, I helped her lift her clean things back into her cart and wheeled them out to her car for her while she carried the baby.

"Thanks for all your help," she said, offering her hand.

"You're welcome," I said, hugging her instead. "I'm glad I met you, Lydia."

"I'm glad, too," she said, and grinned broadly.

I watched from the curb as she drove away, thinking of the Lord's tender mercies.

The next day, the first fast Sunday of the year, I focused my fast on Deb's good health and her beautiful little girl, forgiveness, gratitude for the Savior's love, and gratitude for the change in my heart. I thought about my laundry-day encounter a great deal over the days that followed, pondering the Lord's goodness in my life.

Chapter 8

That Sunday evening, Shari came in fairly late, tiptoed down the hall to put a sleeping Kerry to bed, and then came back into the living room just long enough to say she hoped I wouldn't mind if she wasn't available for our usual family home evening the next night, since she had other plans. I wanted to ask her what was keeping her so busy, but as soon as I said I wouldn't mind missing one FHE, she said, "Thanks!" then was out of the room and down the hall. I didn't see her again that evening or the next morning before I had to leave for school. With my evening free, I decided to go washing machine shopping. (Hint: Same hint as for cars. Monday evenings can be a great time to shop for washers in the Salt Lake Valley.)

I hadn't done much shopping for major appliances before, but I'd brought up the subject in the teachers' lounge during lunch that day, and several people had made good suggestions. By nine o'clock that evening, I had signed away my future for a "mid-range" washer that did just about everything but whistle "Come, Come, Ye Saints" and might have done that if I'd paid a bit extra. As it was, I figured I could just barely pay it off during the six-month interest-free period—if I cut all discretionary buying out of my budget and had a fast day once a week instead of monthly, anyway.

If it hadn't been for Shari and Kerry, I suspect I'd have settled for an old-fashioned wringer washer like my Grandma Kimball used to keep on her back porch—assuming they even made those anymore. I arranged for the washer to be delivered after school the next day and added a few bucks for them to pick up and dispose of the old one. Then I hurried home to tell Shari.

When I found that Shari wasn't back yet, I took a moment to carefully recalculate my budget. With a sense of dread, I realized I had forgotten to deduct the monthly bill for my Internet service. The result was grim: No matter how often I fasted or how little I spent on other things, my budget simply could not stretch far enough to cover payments on the house, car, and washer all at the same time.

I had one brief moment of panic where I almost called the store to cancel the deal. Then I realized that I really didn't have that option, since this had been the least expensive washer that was in stock, and my contract with Shari included laundry access. Besides, I'd come to think of Shari and Kerry almost as family, and I wanted to make things easier for them. I needed Internet access because of my job, so I couldn't cut that out, and I couldn't ask Shari for more rent, since I knew she was just getting by as it was. No matter how I struggled with that budget, it just didn't want to stretch far enough to cover all the expenses I was suddenly building into it.

I worried and fretted for awhile, wondering whether I had been a wicked and slothful servant by allowing myself to get into this much debt in the first place. Finally, feeling miffed at myself for getting into this hole, I scratched a couple of lines into my journal and prepared myself for bed. When I said my prayers, I asked for clarity of thought and vision so I could see a way to meet all my financial obligations, and only then did I begin to feel peace. It was as if I could hear my Heavenly Father saying, "Trust me. I've taken care of you so far."

School that next morning went especially well. Olivia Cantwell gave her first oral book report and did splendidly, despite lacking both front teeth. Jack Sonne and Marcie Russell got into a bit of a squabble over who got to use the beanbag for silent reading but settled it themselves before I could get there. The highlight came when I left one group working in the math center and went to check on the spelling group, only to find Ellen Brenner patiently tutoring Lillian—and Veronica de Guzman and Bao Vang—on the week's word list. This was a third-grade class any teacher would be proud of. I was quite pleased with myself when I took my brown bag into the teachers' lounge.

I walked in on a conversation about Valentine's Day and what various faculty members wanted their classes to do to acknowledge it.

Most of the primary-grade teachers were planning the usual art projects along with having the kids bring valentines to give to everyone in the class. Alicia Despain, who taught fifth grade, plus environmental science units to anyone who would let her, argued that it was a terrible waste of paper to throw away all those valentines every year, but most of the primary-grade teachers defended the practice. "The kids like it," said one of our first-grade teachers, and someone else added that it really helped the students with practicing their letters and their handwriting coordination.

"I'd just as soon forget the whole thing," said Mr. Pastori, who taught sixth grade.

"Yeah, you say that now," Wanda Rice answered, "but that's because you're becoming an old curmudgeon. You did the full mailbox-and-valentine delivery with your classes last year, when you were still married."

"I am not a curmudgeon, just a realist," Pastori answered without heat. I thought that was quite big of him, considering the harshness of the remark, but we had all heard Wanda's scathing, tactless comments before.

I listened for awhile, uncertain of how I felt about the whole valentine thing. When I left the lunchroom some time later, I was fairly certain that I didn't want to do the same old, same old with everyone bringing store-bought valentines, but I couldn't think of a way to make the exercise more meaningful, and when it came right down to it, I felt a little like Mr. Pastori. I'd really have preferred to just cancel the day and forget all about Cupid and the whole hearts-and-flowers routine.

A year ago on Valentine's Day, I'd been planning a May wedding. Although enriched understanding had salved my wounds, I still had to face this year single, without any "prospects" or immediate expectations of finding any. The dearth of romance in my own life made me even more eager to do something different with my class, something much less focused on pair bonds and more far-reaching and . . . what? That was the question.

I finished out the afternoon, which also went better than usual, and found myself stuck a little later than I'd expected to be, talking with Mrs. Russell, who had some concerns about her daughter's social adjustment. I assured her that Lacey was doing well and that these problems were normal for third graders, then rushed home, arriving barely in time to meet the delivery truck.

The delivery guys knew their stuff. Within twenty minutes, the old machine was gone and the new one was installed and operating, and washing my first load of dark colors. Although I still hadn't figured out how to pay for the thing, I was grateful to see it agitating away, answering at least for the moment the question of how Shari and I were going to keep our laundry clean.

Since the clock was edging toward dinner time and it was my week to cook, I started a pot of cricket soup—an old family recipe handed down from a great-grandmother I'd never met, my mother's Grandma Larsen. It was really just a rich potato soup with some browned hamburger and onions thrown in, but the family lore had some great stories about long hours spent "hunting crickets" and guests who blanched when told what was on the menu. With a pan of cornbread and some of Mom's apple butter, it was a satisfying meal, and I already knew that both Shari and Kerry enjoyed it. I had the potatoes boiling and the cornbread started when my housemates came in a half hour later.

"Smells wonderful!" Shari declared as she entered. "Mmm . . . cricket soup, right?"

"Right," I answered. "Welcome home." I put down my spoon and took Shari's book bag so she could help Kerry with her jacket. "Good day at school?"

"Super," she answered. "You too?"

"Super," I answered. "Say, if you're going to be around this evening, I'd like to talk."

"Something serious?" Shari looked concerned, and I realized she probably expected me to raise her rent. I hoped she hadn't worried about it all week.

"Nothing to be afraid of. I just want your advice on what to do with my class for Valentine's Day." I explained my dilemma. Looking relieved, Shari said she'd ponder it and we could talk later. That was when she stepped toward the laundry porch and heard the new washer start its spin cycle, so we had a quick celebration and orientation for the new washing machine.

After dinner, we started into our typical evening routine. Since I had cooked, Shari cleaned up while I read a story to Kerry. Around seven, Shari started the bedtime ritual, and by the time my old clock struck eight, Kerry was settled for the night and we were ready to sit down at the dining table, me with a yellow pad and pencil, and Shari with her thinking cap on. We brainstormed for awhile but weren't coming up with anything. Then Shari said, "What you need is something with a purpose beyond the school, something the kids can do to reach out to someone else."

"Yes, exactly," I answered. "I've even thought of trying to get them involved in a Church-sponsored humanitarian project, but I'm worried about doing something like that in a public school. I need something more general, still with a charitable theme but less specifically Church connected."

"I once heard of a group that made valentines and thank-you cards for American soldiers serving overseas."

"Perfect! That's a great idea! So do you know anyone whose unit is on active duty now?"

"No, sorry. I have a nephew with the Airborne Rangers who was deployed last year, but he's home now. I could do some Internet research when I get some spare time, though. If you have some kind of connection to the people involved, that always makes it feel more personal."

"True. My friend Jeanie had a brother overseas with the army, but I think he's home now. We may have to look around to see if we can find a another connection." Then I paused. "Uh, speaking of spare time," I added, getting around to another subject I had been meaning to bring up, "you don't seem to have had much of that lately. Is it classes or family or maybe . . ." I raised my eyebrows.

Shari grinned. "Well," she said, "it's true that classes are taking a lot of my time this term, but there might be a little 'maybe' thrown in there, too."

"Ah, come on, Shari. Tell me about him," I begged.

"I'm surprised you haven't—" Shari interrupted herself. "That is . . ." She looked away. "Oh, never mind. If things work out the way I hope, you'll know soon enough, anyway."

"Now is soon enough," I hinted. "Know what?" But Shari got out the calendar and started talking about plans for the upcoming month, effectively changing the subject.

"Do you think you might be able to celebrate with us?" she asked. "Kerry is having a birthday next week."

"Really? Next week? Uh, sure, I'd love to!" It simply hadn't occurred to me to ask my new housemates about birthdays, so I was grateful for the heads-up. I got Shari to mark Kerry's birthday on the calendar and then mark her own.

Before I went to bed that evening, I did a little Internet research. I found several groups that organized care packages for troops serving in foreign lands, and a few blogs for individual soldiers or units, but nothing that rang a bell. I also spent a little time at a couple of auction Web sites, looking for possible gifts for Kerry. Since I was already working beyond my budget, I knew I'd have to get creative to find an appropriate gift, yet I couldn't let Kerry's birthday pass unacknowledged. What was the responsible thing to do? It seemed like that question had been on my mind a lot lately, and in a variety of situations.

* * *

Mrs. Brenner, mother of the twins, came to help with reading groups on Thursday. She mentioned that the girls' little sister, Caitlin, was going to be turning three soon, so I asked her about appropriate gifts and mentioned I'd done some looking online.

"You're thinking of vintage gifts, then?" she asked.

"Vintage," I said, considering telling her that I was thinking less of "vintage" and more of "cheap." "Yes. That's kind of what I had in mind."

"The best place to look is your own basement or attic," she said with a knowing air. "That is, assuming you kept any of your old toys."

"I don't . . ." I began, then I thought of some old boxes my mom had put away a few years back. "That just might work."

When I had said good-bye to the kids, I called Mom from the school and asked whether she still had the box with my old toys in it or maybe some toys left from the other girls, and whether she'd mind my coming over to dig through our "vintage" junk.

"Wendy and Denise are out yard-shopping," Mom answered, "so I've got the kids. It's a full house, so I won't be able to help you with anything, but if you're willing to do the digging yourself . . ."

"No problem," I answered. "I'll be right over."

Mom was a gem. Until she mentioned it, I'd forgotten that she watched the kids for Wendy and Denise every Thursday afternoon while they hit the pre-weekend yard sales. A couple of years back, my two sisters-in-law formed a company that bought items at yard sales and flea markets and then resold them online. They didn't earn a lot, but it was enough to give them each a little extra spending cash, they had a lot of fun doing it, and they turned up some pretty good stuff. They couldn't do it without Mom to keep an eye on their little ones, though, and with Timmy, Elise, Audra, and Deirdre all in one place, Mom had her hands more than full whenever she was helping out.

I left school a few minutes later and drove straight over to Mom's. She told me where to look in the rafters over the garage, and I pulled down three big boxes full of old toys. With her permission, I dumped them out in the middle of the family room rug. That way the kids could play with them while Mom and I had a careful look through everything while still keeping an eye on the little ones.

"Kerry's too young for Barbies, isn't she?" I asked as I added a fifth or sixth doll to the pile I'd started. I had been really into Barbies.

"Way too young," Mom agreed. We began stacking all the Barbies in one place and grouping the remaining Lincoln Logs, Tinkertoys, trucks, and so forth in their own respective piles. The scheme didn't work very well, because the kids kept pulling out the toys they liked best and dragging them around the room, but it still allowed us to get some sense of what we had. By the time we got to the bottom of the stack, I'd found a lovely, sweet baby doll that someone had given Ruth right around the time she outgrew baby dolls. This doll was in excellent condition and would be perfect for Kerry. One quick call to Ruth for her okay—readily given—and I had my gift problem solved.

Although I had accomplished my original purpose, the project had taken on a life of its own. As we surveyed the small stacks of old toys that had taken over the family room, Mom suddenly remembered some action figures she'd put away that weren't in the boxes we'd seen so far, so I went back up into the rafters and came down with two more boxes. We were still working through those, talking about who had played with what and how long ago, when Wendy and Denise arrived.

"How'd it go?" Mom asked as they entered the family room.

"Not so good," Wendy answered. "We picked up a couple of old spoons that look like real silver. We'll clean them up and offer them—"

"Hey, what have you got there?" Denise asked, and the two of them zeroed in on our piles of vintage toys. They were especially interested in my stack of old Barbies and started a discussion on which one was Malibu Barbie and which was Career Girl Barbie and which had to be a Twist-n-Turn Barbie, since she had extra joints in her waist, hips, ankles, and knees to allow her to do the Twist, sixties style. I just sat there listening as if eavesdropping on a foreign language. I'd played with the silly things, yet I couldn't remember which doll was which. How could they?

"Oh, Wendy, look at this!" Denise held up a Barbie and Ken doll set still in its original packaging. Like the doll I planned to give to Kerry, this pair had been given to me right around the time I had outgrown Barbies. I must have tucked them into the back of my closet somewhere, since they'd never been passed down to Ruth.

"Are you kidding?" Wendy asked, reverently taking the package Denise handed her. "A Friday Night Dream Date couple! And still in the original package! I can hardly believe it!"

"Look," I said, moving in beside Denise and Wendy. "If you'd like to have some of these, you're welcome to take th—"

"Shh!" Denise said. "Stop right there!" Then Wendy added, "Girl, don't you know what these are *worth?*" For the next several minutes, my two sisters-in-law tried to explain to me about Barbie collectors and fan clubs and the high prices that could be claimed for vintage Barbie dolls. I knew these two women were experienced in the resale business, so I had to take their word for it, but I was a little skeptical. Why would anyone want really old dolls? And the kinds of prices they were talking about seemed way over the top. I mean, who'd pay ninety dollars just to get her hands on an ancient Career Girl Barbie with a raggy briefcase? It seemed way too fantastic to be true.

"Okay," I said finally. "I'll believe you that the dolls are worth something, but I don't know anything about the resale market—"

"Obviously," Denise said with emphasis. "If we weren't family, it would be so easy to take advantage of you!"

"Of course we *wouldn't,*" Wendy added quickly, although there was a twinkle in her eye. "But it sure would be easy . . ."

"Listen," Denise offered. "Why don't we act as your agents? Call it consignment. We'll offer the dolls in our online store and see what happens. If we sell them, we'll take a small commission and bring you the rest. Deal?"

"Sure," I said. "What's a small commission? Thirty percent? Twenty?"

They looked at each other. "Let's say ten," Wendy said, "though I'm not sure you'll want to pay us that much when you see what treasures you have here."

I laughed. "No worries. Ten percent it is. If you make more than a couple of bucks, I'll be surprised."

"Then you'll be surprised," Denise assured me. They loaded the Barbies into one box and started digging through the others, asking Mom if she'd be willing to part with this toy or that one and telling her which they thought would bring the most cash in resale. I listened as they made the same deal with Mom as they'd made with me—a ten percent commission on anything they sold, with the rest going to the original toy owner or, alternatively, to a family fund for play equipment for the grandkids. They promised to get the go-ahead from each family member to avoid selling off any cherished items that would later be missed.

Soon the dealing was done and the two women had picked over all the toys, sorting what they wanted to offer for sale from what would go back into the rafters or into the grandkids' play buckets. As I started to take one of the boxes back to the garage, Wendy called, "Wait!" She lifted one of the action figures off the top. "Is it okay if I take this one too? To keep, I mean?"

Mom answered, "Sure, but what are you going to do with a beat-up army action doll?"

"I think I'll dress him in some new fatigues and send him to my brother, Michael. I told you his unit just got deployed, didn't I?"

"No," Mom answered. "I hadn't heard."

"Me either!" I said eagerly. And that was how I ended up finding the military unit I wanted my students to write to for Valentine's Day. Wendy gave me all the contact information as well as the address for a Web site that had a blog and wish list for Michael's unit. At home that evening, I looked the site up. Michael's unit was new in the arena and just getting used to some fairly strenuous desert war-zone conditions. There were a number of things they needed, or at least wanted very much, that they felt would make their circumstances more homey. When I looked at their wish list, the inspiration began to form. I knew what my class could do.

Chapter 9

We started the next day. I called our endeavor "Project Valentine" and told my students that this year we were going to make our valentines for troops serving overseas. Given the number of soldiers in Michael's outfit, I figured each student would have to make several valentines, but at least we were starting early. With my principal's permission, I made copies of the soldiers' wish list and sent my students home with a note saying that participation was entirely voluntary, but we were collecting items for a Valentine's Day care package. I specified Michael's unit and their field of service and told of my tenuous connection through my sister-in-law. I had thought there might be some interest, but I was wholly unprepared for the deluge of support.

Jordan Warner's father, a dentist, sent enough toothbrushes and sample boxes of toothpaste for every soldier in the unit to have two. Not to be outdone, Henry Jackson's mother, also a dentist, sent twice that many. Dawna Bingham's parents, who operated a small appliance store, sent a couple of large boxes of small batteries—the kind the soldiers could use for flashlights and radios and such—and Mrs. Brenner told me her ward Relief Society had taken on our project and planned to knit black beanies for every soldier in Michael's unit. By the end of the first week, we already had more materials for our basic care packages than I could keep in my classroom, and I had to get the principal's permission to store extra boxes in the library. I began to envision a logistical nightmare. Was I going to have to solicit funds to ship all this stuff?

Wendy stepped in about then, contacting Michael's commanding officer through the blog and telling him what we had going on at the school. Within a few days, she had made arrangements to get the stuff flown over to Michael's guys. All we had to do was deliver it to Hill Air Force Base, marked with the proper delivery info, and the military would take it from there. A few of my students' parents volunteered their pickups for the trip out to Hill, so that took care of the shipping, but the project was growing in other directions as well.

For one thing, Mrs. Jackson, Henry's mom, had suggested that instead of making just the usual heart-shaped valentines cut from red or pink construction paper, we should make life-size paintings of the kids, each with a message to the soldiers written in big red markers in a heart on the child's chest. I imagined this would be an impossible challenge, but she showed me how, by having one of the kids lie still on a large piece of newsprint, another could easily trace around the first. With the kids in pairs, they could create the shapes in an hour, even accounting for mistakes. (For many of the kids, the most difficult part was just lying still!) After the cutouts were made, each child could draw in features however he or she pleased. It was a great idea, and it worked splendidly.

The next development occurred when the other teachers saw what we were doing. Mr. Pastori (alias, The Curmudgeon) was the first to get involved, asking if his students could join our project for their valentines as well. He was followed by the other sixth-grade teachers, then one of the fifth-grade teachers, and by the end of that first week, the principal had approached me to ask if I'd mind making it a project for the entire school. I eagerly agreed, happy to see the kids' Valentine's Day efforts going to a good cause.

The whole school getting involved resulted in more contributions, more boxes full of goodies for the soldiers, and too much stuff for both my classroom and the library. Since I had come up with the idea, I got nominated to haul all the stuff to my garage (my car and Shari's got to spend the rest of January in the driveway), and then find and purchase enough brightly colored tempera paints for the whole school to use.

During the first week of Project Valentine, I took a couple of evenings away from the endeavor to help Shari plan a birthday party for Kerry. We invited some of Kerry's friends from her preschool, as well as a few children from her Primary class. Shari made Kerry's favorite caramel fudge cake with coconut icing and baked it in cupcakes so the kids could each have their own. She insisted they eat on the laundry porch, just to avoid messing up the house. I gave Kerry the baby doll I had saved for her, and she acted like it was the greatest gift ever.

I was feeling pretty good about myself until Noah arrived in Seth's pickup and unloaded a full-sized swing set for the backyard. When I said, "You're showing me up, brother," he assured me that he had bought it second-hand and had gotten a very good deal. But still . . . a swing set? And in January? I stared in disbelief as he unloaded it piece by piece and set it up, all the while assuring me that it was also portable, so Kerry could take it with her whenever she and her mother moved. That caused a bit of a stab to my heart, since I hadn't thought of them leaving and realized I didn't want them to.

There were other gifts, too, though none from Kerry's father, but I didn't think she even noticed. She had such a wonderful time; she must have known she was a much-loved little lady.

A few nights after Kerry's party, I gathered a group of volunteers at my place to package and label everything going to the troops. It had been something of a whirlwind effort to get everything together that far in advance of *the day,* but our Air Force contacts assured us that we had to ship everything out early to be sure the supplies would reach the soldiers by February fourteenth.

Shari and Kerry got home early that night and helped me scoot the kitchen table to the side, creating more work space. Four of my class parents, three of the school's teachers, and a couple of student teachers all showed up, along with Wendy, Denise, Noah, Mom, and Ruth, who said she had just popped up for the evening but was glad to help with the "family" project.

We made quite an eclectic ensemble—the sixteen of us spread out across the floor—but we organized ourselves into work teams, and things quickly fell into place. Denise and Wendy had ordered boxes from the company they used for shipping resale items, Noah had used his home computer to generate copies of the Air Force shipping label with the proper military identifiers, and Shari had gathered up used

Styrofoam "popcorn" packing material from the education department office at the BYU extension campus, where she was taking most
of her classes. Mr. Pastori had brought several large rolls of packing
tape he had purchased on sale at an office supply store. With plenty
of volunteer labor to use it all, we were good to go.

It took some coordination to get everything sorted and packed,
but we had a good, organized crew, and it came together well. When
we finished the packing a little before 10:00 P.M., we had enough boxes
to fill three pickup trucks, which made me glad Denise had driven my
brother Seth's pickup and was willing to help haul things to the school.

Two things happened that evening that ultimately had interesting
consequences, though neither seemed to be that big a deal at the
time. The first occurred just as the party began breaking up and Mrs.
Decker, one of the fourth-grade teachers at my school, called her
daughter to come and pick her up. Her daughter, Mary Alice, arrived
with a camera and a small tape recorder and asked permission to take
pictures—and by the way, would I mind giving her an interview?

"What for, Mary Alice?" I asked her.

"I'm a journalism major at the U," she replied. "I can use it for
class, or maybe for my internship."

So I gave her a brief interview and smiled when she took pictures
of our small work group in front of a room full of boxes.

The other incident began just as simply. Just as I was trying to
make sure the last of the boxes were all properly labeled, Ruth started
in again on Mormons2Marry.com. I was feeling brain-drained and
not much in the mood to be nagged about anything, least of all the
computer dating service Ruthie had set me up with.

"I haven't got time now, Ruth," I barked.

"So when *will* you have time? You don't want me to feel like you
don't appreciate my gift, do you?"

I rolled my eyes. "Puh-lease. I haven't even had a chance to fill out
my part of the survey."

"Then let's do it now." The girl simply would *not* take a hint.

"Ruth, I'm busy!"

"But I'm not," she said, sounding oh so reasonable. "Look. I've
got the form right here online. You go on checking labels, and I'll just
ask you a few simple questions. It'll be done before you know it."

"Ruth . . ." I began. But I know when I'm beaten. "Okay," I said, finally out of ammunition. "Uh, whenever you're ready, I guess." Then I went on checking labels while Ruth mumbled to herself, filling in the blanks on the first part of the application with information she already knew about me, like my name, birth date, address, and so forth.

"Age range?" she asked after a minute.

"Uh, for the potential dates, you mean?"

"Uh, duh. Ye-ah."

"No more than one year younger or four older," I said with conviction, adding extra tape to a label that had come loose.

Ruth hesitated, frowned, then sighed and typed in my answer. "You're getting kind of picky, aren't you?"

"Not really. I'm just thinking of a couple of guys I've met who are twenty-seven or twenty-eight and *way* too old for me. And anyone more than a year younger is probably still dealing with post-missionary distress syndrome. A big *no thanks* on that!"

Ruth grimaced but didn't argue. "So, any other parameters you want me to set?"

I thought of Aunt Lizbeth and used cars. "Just tell the computer not to set me up with anyone who's been divorced," I said.

Ruth's brow furrowed. "You could be weeding out some great guys . . ."

I bit my lip to keep from scowling. I didn't want *any* of this, so why did I have to justify my silly snap decisions? I simply growled, "Why buy someone else's problems?"

There was a sharp sweep of air, and a door slammed in the back of the house. "Drafty old place," I complained.

Ruth whispered, "Are you sure that wasn't Shari?"

I shook my head. "Shari left with the first truckload. It was just the wind."

"I'm not sure," Ruth said, still whispering. "You might want to check—"

"Let's just get this *done*, okay?"

"It's done already." Ruth pressed the ENTER key with a flourish. "All you have to do now is log on to see which introductions the computer has picked for you. If you like, I could check for you this evening, after we get the rest of the boxes delivered."

"Yeah, sure. Uh, thanks, sis." *Oh, boy!* I thought sarcastically. But I knew I had that one coming after putting Ruth off for so long. I reminded myself to try to be more pleasant when she looked up my potential dates later that evening.

It was time to haul the last of the boxes over to the school, so the last of our volunteers helped while I supervised the loading of Seth's truck. Then Noah and I crowded into the cab beside Denise, and we all headed for the school, leaving Mom and Ruth to clean up after us. No sooner had I packed in next to Noah than I began to quiz him about his experiences with Mormons2Marry.com and what I could expect. "Really, Noah, do you think there's any value in this for me?"

Denise gave a deep, exaggerated sigh, but I ignored her. So what if my family had heard all this before? I was nervous about it, or I'd have done it sooner. "Really," I said again. "Come on, Noah."

Noah seemed to be measuring his words. "It's tough to say, sis. My membership hasn't turned up any marriage prospects, but then again, I know a few great couples who met through Internet dating services and—"

"You haven't been on your last date, have you?"

"You mean my fifth introduction?"

"Whatever. You still have one left, right?"

"Well, yes, but—"

"So why aren't you taking full advantage? I mean, if it's such a good deal for me, then maybe—"

"Okay, okay," Noah answered, sounding beleaguered. "I'll make you a deal. If you promise you'll accept your first introduction by this weekend, I'll sign up for my last one." He sighed. "I hope that makes you feel better."

I paused. "Okay," I said, finally out of excuses.

By this time, we were almost at the school. After unloading and hauling and stacking the materials, we placed them in the cafeteria and got into the truck again. Noah pushed me to the middle, beside Denise, which was when I remembered I still had unfinished business with her, too.

"I don't suppose you've had any nibbles on my old dolls," I said.

"You'd be surprised," Denise said.

"That's what you always say."

"And it's true," she answered. "Wendy and I will have a check for you next Monday."

"No kidding! Already?" She had been right; I was surprised.

"No kidding," she answered and pulled up in front of my house, where she stopped just long enough to let Noah and me get out before heading home to Seth and her babies.

"How big a check?" I called as she drove away, but she just shouted, "See you at the family gathering on Sunday!"

I arrived inside to find Ruth hovering over the computer. "So are you ready to sign in and see if you have any introductions?"

It took a bit of effort to summon a smile. "Thanks, Ruth. What's my online identifier?"

"You'll see," she said with an air of mystery. "But you'll like it, I'm sure."

"So how will I know . . . ?"

But Ruth was already typing. "Um, nothing yet," she reported, "but by tomorrow your e-mail will have several possible profiles that the computer has matched you up with. Your new login ID will be on all the e-mails that come from the company."

"Okay. I guess that will be hard to miss," I said, wondering if I could think of a way to miss it without ticking off both Ruth and Noah. "By the way, where did Noah go?" I asked, looking around.

"He's in the kitchen, of course." Ruth smiled and shook her head as if anyone could have guessed that.

I stepped into the kitchen to find Mom sweeping the floor. Shari was rinsing up the cups and small plates we had used for refreshments for our work crew, and Noah was drying them and putting them into the cupboard. Mom was narrowing down her little dirt pile, so I grabbed the dust pan and hurried over to make myself useful.

Mom and Ruth left a few minutes later, but only after Ruth had extracted a solemn promise that I would respond to someone's profile before I went to bed the next night. Not long after that, Noah announced that he needed to leave as well, and didn't Shari want her things that she had left in his car? I wondered when she might have left things in his car, but Shari nodded and said yes, she did want those things, and put on her heavy coat so she could go outside with Noah.

It was late, and I had school the next morning, so I went to my room to get ready for bed. I jotted a few lines in my journal, then spent a little time on my nightly ritual of washing and moisturizing my face and brushing my teeth. I came out in my jammies, ready to do my nightly locking-up rounds. That was when Shari came through the front door and I jumped as if bee-stung. "Shari, you startled me!"

Shari jumped as high as I had, her face flushing bright red. "You startled me, too! I thought you knew I was out there."

"Sorry, I thought . . . Shari, are you okay?" She had been outside so long, and she looked so shaken, her face so red.

"Oh, yes! Um, yes. Well, good night, Sarah," she called as she walked down the hall. "I hope you're happy with the way your project turned out."

"Yes, I am. Very happy. But Shari . . . ?"

But Shari was already stepping into her room before I could ask her whether she'd been able to get her things from Noah's car. I shrugged. She must not have, because she had come in empty-handed.

* * *

School that next day went smoothly, and Project Valentine appeared to be a great success. During the assembly when the whole student body turned out to applaud themselves for the three truckloads of "valentines" they were sending overseas, Mrs. Decker's daughter even showed up again, this time with a cameraman in tow. She used a more sophisticated tape recorder this time, sticking the microphone in the faces of some of the children and jotting down good quotes from other teachers. But soon enough, it was all over, and the three parents who had offered their trucks showed up to haul everything out to the Air Force base as promised. I watched them go with relief, glad to have the project over and done with, but just as glad that we'd started it. It had been a positive way for the kids to channel their excitement about the coming celebration.

Valentines were very much on my mind when I returned home that evening. Though I looked forward to checking my e-mail the way a condemned man might anticipate his walk to the gallows, I steeled myself to sit down at the computer as soon as I got home. I'd promised Ruth I would, after all, and I'd practically twisted Noah's arm to make him promise he'd suffer with me, so it only seemed fair to follow through on my end.

Shari wasn't home from school yet, so it was just me and the computer when I sat down, took a deep breath, and logged on to my e-mail. As Ruth had promised, there was a message from Mormons2Marry.com. It was addressed to BrunetteBeauty (I made a mental note to beat Ruth soundly) and came complete with a batch of profiles of "possible intros" the site could arrange for me. My job was to narrow them down to only one.

I found it wasn't easy. Computer security is a great thing, but these profiles said so little about the guys, it was hard to know whether I was reading about someone I'd actually want to meet or not. I decided to begin with those I could easily weed out, like HeartOfGold, who was described as "forty-two, fit, and fine." Fine for someone else, maybe, but forty-two was a little out of my age range. I wondered if Ruth had really set the parameters I had asked for, or if the computer had just ignored them.

I also eliminated DaffyDuck, strictly because I was sure I didn't want to date anyone who would use that alias, then weeded out ArchimedesPrinciple for similar reasons. DoesWindows sounded handy enough, but he was also past forty, as was BodyMechanic. (I briefly wondered about this one. Was he a physical therapist? A plastic surgeon? Maybe he worked on car bodies? But he was forty-five, and I wasn't curious enough to find out.)

After eliminating that first batch, I found it easier to narrow down other possibilities. Once I had cut out anyone more than four years older than I was, and *everyone* who had been divorced, it was easy to cut the list to two. Of those two, I found I was more curious about the one called LostArkGuy. My brothers are all big *Indiana Jones* fans. The Christmas before last, Noah had bought Mark the original *Indiana Jones* trilogy. So it seemed reasonable to me that anyone who was a "Lost Ark guy" would probably be an enjoyable date—at least for the one time we would have to meet. I completed the form, asking for my first introduction to LostArkGuy, and went ahead with checking the rest of my e-mail, glad to have that little trial over with.

When I got home from school the next day, I had a response from Mormons2Marry.com saying that LostArkGuy was interested in meeting me, too, so I filled out the little form that said when and where (that is, in which "sector" of the valley) I'd be willing to meet him and sent it right in.

Within minutes, I had another message back from the company—and a date. LostArkGuy must have been online at the same time I was. The message said that Saturday lunch was good for him, too, and that we could meet at the little French bakery near my home, which served sandwiches and salads. I responded, "How will I know you?" and moments later had the response, "There's a florist right near there, so I'll be the guy with the yellow rose." I had to admit that brought me a smile, and I began to think I might actually like LostArkGuy. Still communicating through the Mormons2Marry.com Web site, we agreed on Saturday at eleven-thirty, and I went through the evening humming, happy to discover that I was actually looking forward to a date for the first time since Justin.

* * *

As the weekend drew near, I found myself wishing I had a little something to spend—partly to celebrate what a good week I'd had at school and partly because it would have been fun to go shopping for something new and pretty—a new red dress, maybe—to wear on my date. However, since there wasn't enough cash to cover what I had already spent, I settled for pressing my dressy charcoal slacks and airing out the cashmere sweater.

I fretted and fussed my way through Saturday morning, making such a nuisance of myself that Shari finally said, "Sarah, it's just a date, for heaven's sake!"

"I know," I answered, "but what if he's awful?"

"Then you only have a half hour or so of 'awful' to get through," she replied. "You're really more concerned that he might be great, aren't you?"

I wrinkled my nose. "You know, you're way too perceptive."

"I've just come to know you pretty well, my friend." Shari sat down beside me at the kitchen table. "You desperately want to fall in love again, and you're afraid that it might really happen."

"You're onto me, all right," I said. "Or is it just that you know the whole routine because it's familiar to you, too?"

"Touché," Shari answered. "You're right, of course."

"What a pair we make!" I smiled. "So, when are you going to tell me about the late nights you've been keeping?"

She looked away. "Really, there's nothing to tell—at least, not yet."

"Ah, come on, Shari." I didn't realize I was drumming my fingers on the table until Shari gently laid her hand over mine.

"It's going to be okay," she said. "Look. It's almost time to go."

I looked at the clock and saw she was right. Somehow the last hour had actually gone by, and it was time to put on my lipstick and head for Chalet Francaise. "Wish me luck?" I asked as I opened the garage door.

Shari grinned. "You don't need any."

That held me together until I got to the bakery; however, I thought about turning around and driving home as soon as I arrived there. *What if . . .* But Shari was right and I knew it. My greatest fear was that LostArkGuy would turn out to be wonderful and that I wouldn't be ready for him yet. The only way to find out was to forge ahead. I found a parking place, took a deep breath, and went inside.

It was one of those crisply cold, bright winter days, and it took my eyes a moment to adjust to the relative darkness inside the café. Then I looked around, and the first person I saw was—

"Sarah? What are you doing here?" Noah stood. That was when I realized he was holding a yellow rose.

"Oh, no! You're LostArkGuy!"

His jaw dropped. "And you're BrunetteBeauty. I should have known!"

For a moment we both stood there, looking stunned. All I could say was, "I'm going to kill Ruth."

There was another moment of total, embarrassed silence. Then Noah started laughing. It was a little laugh at first, and then a belly laugh, and then something more like a horse laugh. As I watched him, I finally saw the humor in our situation and began laughing, too.

"C'mere, sis," Noah said after a minute, and he held out his arms. I walked into the hug. Then we hugged and held each other and laughed until we cried while the café's other patrons looked on in bemused silence.

Chapter 10

Shari laughed too when I told her about my "date" an hour later. I was touched that she looked so relieved. I decided I felt the same way—at least I hadn't come home with a horror story about meeting Ron-the-Sequel. We agreed it would be better if Ruth didn't hear about this—at least not from either of us—and Noah had already sworn he wouldn't tell. I knew Ruth would be asking by the time we were all together at Mom and Dad's the next day, so I promised myself that my answer would be truthful—just not complete. I'd say something like, "He was a great guy, and we had a good time, but I don't think I'll be dating him again." If pressed, I'd tell her there was "no romantic spark." Talk about an understatement! Maybe I could tell her that hugging him felt a lot like hugging my brother. Whatever I said, I wouldn't tell her what had happened. Despite the slight urge to gloat over Mormons2Marry.com's first strike—I mean, how many people get set up with their siblings? The site definitely needed some kind of filter it didn't currently have—I knew Ruth would feel bad about what had happened, and I didn't want to hurt her feelings.

I enjoyed church the next day—all of it. Before attending our own meetings, Shari and I drove across the valley to see Lauren blessed in Deb and Brian's ward. We stayed for part of their fast and testimony meeting, too. It was moving to hear Deb bear her testimony, sharing her gratitude for just being alive and able to be with us. Brian bore a touching testimony, too, though when he tried to talk about that awful night when we almost lost Deb, he broke down and had to cut to a quick ending. We'd have stayed for the whole meeting except that Kerry got fussy, and Shari feared she wouldn't be able to make it through our own ward's full schedule if we didn't take time to get her a snack. We stopped by the house to get half a peanut butter sandwich for Kerry on the way to meet with our own ward.

Our ward's fast and testimony meeting was also inspiring. The bishop opened it by testifying of the importance of personalizing the Lord's Atonement. I felt the Spirit so strongly then and knew I needed to get up, so I rose as soon as the bishop turned the time over to the congregation. I tried to keep my testimony brief, just giving thanks for the gospel and the Atonement and telling the ward how grateful I was for the miracles on behalf of my sister and her baby girl. The other experiences, the ones dealing with Kyle and forgiveness, were way too personal to share. Still, I choked up as I bore testimony of the Lord's grace and of His power in my life.

When church was over, we arrived back home in a rush with just enough time to get changed and dressed and to pick up the food we'd prepared the day before—my usual fruit salad and another of Shari's decadent caramel fudge cakes. (I was pretty sure I could gain three pounds just breathing in the same room with that cake.) Then we were off again, on our way to the monthly Kimball gathering.

Sometime in the next few minutes, around the time we crossed the Jordan, it occurred to me that including Shari and her daughter in the family gatherings had become so natural that I hardly even thought about it anymore. It seemed right for them to be with us at Lauren's blessing and at the monthly dinner. I thought of what Noah had said about the swing set being easy to move and wondered what would happen in the coming months, once Shari got her credentials and a real teaching job. I was still thinking about this when we arrived at my parents' home.

We were a little early this time, so much of the family hadn't arrived yet, but Noah was there, and Kerry ran to meet him, shouting "Noah! Noah!"

"Hey there, sweetheart!" he called. He lifted her in the air and swung her around, then kissed her before setting her on her feet again. He helped her with her coat and then helped Shari with hers, and I again thought about how my roommates had become so well integrated into my whole family.

Dinner went smoothly, although, as predicted, I did have to dodge some of Ruth's questions about my first computer date. She accepted my explanations about "no romantic spark," but told me she'd call the next weekend to see how my next date went. I got around that one by telling her I was going to be pretty busy for a few days. She frowned but let it go with the comment, "Soon though, right?"

"Uh, yeah. Right," I replied, deciding I'd figure out how to dodge the next bullet later.

Just before we served dessert, Mom and Dad stood at the head of the table, and Dad tapped his glass for our attention. "We're going to do something unusual this year," he began and turned to Mom, who said, "Valentine's Day is a week from Wednesday. We know that isn't a convenient time for most of you, given work and school schedules and such, but we'd like to have all of you come to dinner here that evening, if you can make it."

"We want to share that time with all our Valentines," Dad said and smiled. Mom smiled too, but the way they looked at each other and the little twinkle in their eyes told me there was something more that they weren't saying—at least not yet. I pondered this while we ate Shari's marvelous cake, but I couldn't for the life of me imagine what kind of surprise they might be saving for Valentine's Day. However, I did think of an idea for a Valentine's surprise of my own.

The next day at lunch, Mr. Pastori mentioned that we'd finished Project Valentine so early that the kids were asking what the class would get to do for the *real* Valentine's Day.

I piped up. "My students are making valentines to take home to their parents and family—sort of "thank-you" cards for the people they love most."

"Life-size again?" he asked.

"Sure, why not?" I said. The idea buzzed around the teachers' lounge, and before I knew it, most of the school planned on making more life-size valentines with straight-from-the-heart messages, this time for the kids' own families.

I had just gotten back from Allie's Art Mart for more valentine supplies when Wendy and Denise stopped by for a surprise visit. Wendy ceremoniously presented me with a check for an amount so large I thought they must be joking. "Is this for real?" I asked, counting the digits in *front* of the decimal point.

"Absolutely," Denise assured me. "Told ya those dolls were valuable."

"Of course, that includes the profits from your Easy Bake Oven, too," Wendy added.

"But this check. It's . . . it's huge!"

"Well, if you don't want it . . ." Wendy made a grab.

I yanked it away. "Not on your life!!" I looked at it again. "You didn't accidentally misplace the decimal or something?"

"No, that's the correct amount," Denise said. They were both grinning like jack-o-lanterns.

"You already took out your commission and everything?"

"Ten percent," Wendy said, "just like we agreed."

"Wow," I said again and put the check in my pocket.

My two sisters-in-law high-fived each other as they turned to leave. Over her shoulder, Denise said loudly, "She sure would have been easy to con."

"Sure would have," Wendy said. They grinned and waved as they left me standing in my kitchen, still hardly believing what had just happened.

Earlier that day, Shari had left a message letting me know that she and Kerry had plans for the evening, and so it was that after dinner I found myself alone in the living room, quietly thumbing through old copies of the *Ensign*. Out of habit, I turned to the art on the inside covers, hoping to find a copy of *Embrace,* or perhaps another painting by the same artist, in addition to the one I'd already found in the January issue.

I did find one painting from several months earlier. It featured a laughing Savior tossing a little child in the air the way I had seen Noah toss Kerry at the family dinner on Sunday. Other young children stood around the Savior, all of them looking up toward Him with joy, admiration, and love. As in the other paintings, the human figures were almost photographic in their realism while the background was more abstract, a suggestion of a busy street scene, perhaps on market day. Again, the painting reached me directly, a kind of Spirit-to-spirit message. The longer I admired it the more I felt I understood the Savior. It was a moment of perfect peace—one that I would reflect on many times during the emotional roller coaster of the weeks that followed.

Chapter 11

Tuesday was one of the high points of the week. On my way to school that next day, I stopped by an ATM and deposited my "Barbie check." It wasn't like it was going to pay off the national debt or even my slightly more modest home mortgage, but it was certainly the answer to my worries about current expenses. I even stopped at the appliance store on my way home and paid off—completely paid off!—my new washer. I couldn't help remembering how the still, small voice had whispered, "Trust me." I knew I had seen an answer to my prayers. I even went by the bank and shifted a little cash into my savings account—the first time money had gone in and not out in nearly a year. I grinned. I'd forgotten the power of having a little cash.

On Friday, my euphoria from the Barbie windfall was replaced with worry when I discovered that one of my students, Emily Ruskin, had been in a bad traffic accident that left Emily, her two brothers, and her mother hospitalized. Emily was listed in "serious, but stable" condition, as was her mother, but her older brothers, Trevor and Ty, Mr. Pastori's students, were both critical—and it wasn't looking good. We were careful in how we presented the news to the children, but it was a hard blow for everyone. Many people volunteered to pray for the Ruskin family, and even though we couldn't organize anything official—since we were a public school—I assured everyone who asked that the Ruskins would appreciate their prayers.

When one of the LDS mothers organized a phone tree on her own and invited anyone who wished to join an organized fast, I was grateful that someone not directly connected to the school had done so. I willingly promised to fast again that Sunday. So did most of our school families—Catholics, Baptists, Protestants, and Evangelicals included. We were even joined by our one Muslim and two Buddhist families.

It was a relief that following Monday to learn that Emily and her mom were both home from the hospital—battered, but healing—and that her brothers had been upgraded to "serious" and were no longer in critical care. When Mr. Salazar made the announcement on the PA system, the whole school broke into spontaneous applause. We could hear the cheering from the sixth-grade class across the yard from us. I said a silent prayer, thanking Heavenly Father for His love and mercy.

The following day we finished our second batch of valentines-from-the-heart, and Mary Alice Decker showed up with her camera again, asking if she could shoot pictures in my classroom. Mr. Salazar had checked her in through the office and given her appropriate passes, and the kids seemed eager to talk about what they had done, so I invited her in again. By now, I doubted that anything would come of these interviews, but I still answered all her questions as well as I could and even managed to work in the name of the art supply store—as thanks for the price breaks they'd given us.

That afternoon, the kids carefully accordion-folded their life-size self-portraits and tucked them into big envelopes we had made during art class. Then they addressed them to their families and took them home, planning to present them before school on the big day. Little did we know the *Deseret News* would beat them to the punch.

I first heard about it when I was pulling out of my driveway the next morning and Mrs. Wyatt, my neighbor from across the street, called out, "Congratulations!" When I asked for what, she called, "Saw your picture on the front page!"

Feeling certain we were dealing with a case of mistaken identity, I smiled politely and drove to school—where everyone I saw waved or greeted me expansively. When the front office staff applauded as I walked in to check my mailbox, I said, "Okay, what's going on?"

"You haven't seen it?" Mrs. Olson asked from behind the front desk.

"Seen what?"

That was when she and Tiffany, our attendance clerk, produced the morning paper. There I was on the front page, holding up a life-size self-portrait of Henry Jackson, with Henry himself posing next to it. The story was headlined, "School Children Give Soldiers Their Hearts" and was credited to Mary Alice Decker, *Deseret News* intern.

A few paragraphs appeared beside the large photo, and then the story continued inside, where there were more pictures of the kids, the school, and the three truckloads of boxes we'd assembled. The report ended with a couple of paragraphs about the Valentine's Day greetings we'd made for the kids' families and quotations from a few of the younger children saying things like, "My mom is my favorite valentine" or "I love my daddy." I had to admit that Mary Alice had done us proud. The story looked great, but I was embarrassed that so much of the attention had landed on me. The idea had grown so organically, had been such an amalgam of different people's help and suggestions, that it felt wrong to take the credit. I thanked Mrs. Olson and Tiffany and hurried to my classroom, eager to duck further attention.

But the attention followed me. Throughout the day, kids, teachers, staff, and even parents hunted me down to tell me how great the story had been and how pleased they all were with the results of Project Valentine. The school kids had been pretty good about keeping the surprise of their from-the-heart valentines, so many parents had been surprised that morning—either by their own children or the morning paper.

As the day went on, it became clear that something special had happened in our school community. We'd pulled together for the soldiers, then the Ruskins, and then our families. Any differences among us seemed insignificant in light of our common concern for others. We were experiencing a sense of unity unlike anything I'd felt before—my own family and ward aside, anyway. It felt good just to be part of it.

The surprises continued at the afternoon assembly-combination-party when, just before the room parents brought out their usual sugary treats, Mr. Salazar called me up in front of the student body and presented me with a trophy. It was small, just intended as a token, but it came from our parent-teacher organization, and it meant a great deal to me. It was about nine inches tall, with a base of polished wood some five inches high. On the base was the figure of a woman wearing a long skirt. She was bending as if reaching down, perhaps toward a small child, smiling encouragement, her hand outstretched. On the base was a large heart with the inscription, "To Miss Sarah Kimball, straight from our hearts."

Some of the sixth graders started shouting, "Speech, speech, speech," and Mr. Salazar handed me the microphone. I couldn't think of anything to say. I gulped, choked down tears, and finally said, "You *all* deserve this. Thank you." The school cheered wildly, and I hoped they were cheering for themselves. It was humbling and uncomfortable and an absolutely great—no, make that wonderful—surprise.

A second surprise came immediately after, when one of our class parents showed up with a small bouquet, which she and her son presented to me on behalf of the whole class. I clutched my trophy and my flowers, grinning with embarrassed delight.

As Mr. Salazar made his last announcement, closing the assembly and ending the school day, I was immediately surrounded by well-wishers who wanted to congratulate me—and by a huge cloud of self-doubt. If I'd done anything at all, it was to act on other people's good ideas. Being the center of attention—at least, for this reason—just didn't seem fair.

As I was trying to make my way past half a dozen parents who wanted to shake my hand, I suddenly remembered what I'd been thinking just a few hours earlier. In a flash of clarity, I understood that all this attention really *wasn't* all about me. It was about the wonderful sense of unity and oneness we'd had in our school community lately. I'd spoken nothing less than the truth when I told the school assembly that *they* deserved the trophy, and somehow they had known it. They were feeling good about *themselves*—about their own acts of generosity and love—and they needed a focal point for expressing those feelings.

As these thoughts filled my mind, the Spirit spoke again, replacing unease with peace. I slowed my step, spending a little time with each well-wisher, shaking their hands, telling them how much I'd appreciated their help and their children's efforts, and doing what I could to help them feel the joy of all they had accomplished. I knew then that in congratulating me, they were enjoying a bit of that moment of joy in their own lives. It was worth taking some time and making some effort to help them share that sweet reward.

Chapter 12

I was a little later than I had hoped to be in getting packed up and off the school grounds, so I was sure Shari would be home by the time I got there. I felt eager to share my trophy—and my new understanding of success and appreciation—with her. I parked my car in the garage, then entered the kitchen, calling, "Shari, you home?"

There was no answer, but I only had to take a few more steps before I saw the sign taped to the cupboard door: "I've gone ahead to your parents' house. Please come as soon as you can. Hugs, Shari."

Disappointment washed through me, bitter to the taste. Shari had been gone so much lately. Couldn't she have been here for me on this one big, important day? I dropped down into one of the dinette chairs, pushed the trophy to the back of the table, and sighed. *Nothing to be done about it now. Better get over to the big Valentine's Day dinner.* Then, trying not to feel so petty, I touched up my lipstick and headed toward my parents' home.

I arrived to find the whole gang in the family room, gathered in front of the TV—definitely not the Kimball norm. "Hey, guys! What's up?" I said.

Timmy said, "Shh, Auntie Sarah!" and Wendy said, "Join us, Sarah. It's almost time."

"Almost time for what?" I asked, but then I looked at the screen and saw a KSL reporter standing in front of my school.

"Here," Ruth said, and patted the spot on the couch beside her. I sat.

There we were, the lead story on the Valentine's Day newscast. They showed the picture of Henry Jackson and his life-size paper doll, with me grinning beside him, a few minutes of video footage from the assembly, and a quick interview with my principal, who gave me credit for the whole project.

The story came complete with a live feed from a TV crew overseas. There on the screen were Wendy's brother Mike and the soldiers of his unit, all wearing black hand-knitted beanies, holding up life-size images of the kids from our school, and waving and blowing kisses at the camera and shouting, "Happy Valentine's Day!" It probably would have made me teary-eyed even if it hadn't been our soldiers and our school and our kids.

As the segment ended, my family began to applaud, and I got even tearier.

"That was great!" my dad said as he clicked off the set. "Congratulations, honey!" He lifted me into a giant bear-hug.

Everyone else wanted a hug, too. When I'd finished the rounds, I asked, "So, how long have you guys known about this? And when were you going to tell me?"

"You didn't know?" Noah asked. He looked at Shari, who was sitting beside him. She looked stricken. I felt another black mark go up next to Shari's name on the big Behavior Blackboard in my mind. Could you keep a roommate in during recess?

"The principal said he was going to announce it today," Shari said apologetically. "I thought surely—"

"Wait, wait," I said reluctantly, finally remembering. "He did make an announcement about something at the end of the assembly, but I missed what he said."

"Then I'm glad you got here in time," Mom said.

I decided to let it go. "The TV story was cool, huh?" I said, and the momentary unease passed.

For the next few minutes my family filled me in on the contacts Wendy had made with Mike's commanding officer, the calls from the news station, and a couple weeks' worth of quiet, behind-the-scenes planning. Then Dad began moving furniture, setting up the two extra folding tables and the chairs we use whenever the whole family gets together. *Okay,* I thought, *I've had my fifteen minutes of fame and it's time to get down to business.* I joined the others who had started pitching in, helping to get everything ready. I let the guys set up the chairs while I went into the kitchen to see if I could help with the food.

I entered to hear Ruth telling Mom about a study she had just been reading about in one of her sociology classes on gendered instruction in math and science. That subject had interested me for awhile, so I hung around the kitchen, setting out food and listening to Ruth explain to Mom how concepts could be presented in ways more attuned to how boys and men, or girls and women, learn. Ruth shared insights from the study while I dished up soup and prepared salad and appetizer courses. I noticed that there had certainly been a lot of fine food prepared.

"What's up, Mom?" I asked when Ruth stepped away. "We never get this fancy, not even for Christmas."

Mom grinned. "Something special for our many sweet valentines," she said, but I saw that mischievous grin again. There was more going on here than she was saying, but I knew she wouldn't say a word until she was ready. Sighing, I followed her to the tables, carrying two pitchers of ice water.

Dad began our feast by blessing the food and giving thanks for "a day when we can celebrate the love we share, and the blessing of eternal marriage." After the prayer, Ruth and Shari served the appetizer course, Wendy and Denise followed with the soup and salad, and then Mom and I brought out the entrée and side dishes. For the finale of our feast, Noah served up the dessert—a marvelous chocolate torte I recognized from Chalet Francaise, topped with piping hot sweet cherries. I looked at the decadent spread, puzzled. Mom and Dad never spent this lavishly on a big family meal. What was going on here? Just then, Dad stood and tapped his glass until the usual din subsided.

"I guess you're all wondering why I called this meeting," he began, and a light titter went around the table, along with a shiver of expectancy.

Then Noah stood. "Actually, Dad didn't really call it at all. *I* called this meeting. That is, *we* called it."

He took Shari's elbow. She jumped out of her chair and flashed a shiny diamond ring. "We're engaged!"

There was a burst of cheers and applause, and then the room started to buzz. I heard Deb say, "I knew it!"

"Well it's about time," Wendy added.

Someone else said, "Wow! The family just keeps growing!"

Then a harsh voice shouted, "NO-O-O-O!" and all conversation ceased. It wasn't until I noticed my whole family staring at me in stunned silence that I recognized the shout had been mine. "That is, uh, I mean, I . . . didn't know."

It was Mom who answered, her voice gentle. "Sweetheart, I thought you'd seen this coming."

"I guessed it weeks ago," Denise said, and the buzz in the room slowly began to rise again while I sank into my chair. Though family members were still tossing me cautious looks, and Shari was flatly refusing to look at me, the chat level quickly rose once more, as each member of the family came around the table to hug Noah and welcome Shari into the family.

I watched for a few moments and then excused myself to use the bathroom, hoping I could get down the hallway before the tears started splashing down my cheeks. I felt hurt, angry, and betrayed. He was my brother, she my roommate and dear friend. *Why hadn't they said anything?*

I sat in the bathroom, dabbing at tears and making more, then dabbing them up again as I thought of all the times I had tried to get Shari to talk about her late evenings. I remembered how hesitant Noah had been to go on his last computer date and how relieved Shari had seemed when that date had turned out to be me. They must have had an understanding even then.

Before then, I realized, as I remembered Noah telling me weeks ago that he thought he might want to find someone on his own, and Sherry admitting to having a romantic interest. I thought about that day at the pizza parlor and the way Kerry had shouted, "Noah! Noah!" as she ran into his arms at our last family dinner, just days before. I realized that this had been happening for *weeks,* right under my nose, and no one had said a thing. I felt bitterly betrayed and blind and foolish; I felt awful.

I was halfway into a full-blown sobbing pity party when someone knocked on the door. I choked down the knot in my throat and called out a shaky, "Just a minute."

"Sarah, it's Mom." There was a no-nonsense tone in her voice. "Sarah, open the door."

"I'll be just a minute," I repeated.

"Open the door now."

I had heard that tone before. I meekly opened the door. Mom stepped in and closed it behind her. "Sarah, what on earth is the matter with you?"

"I . . . I don't know, Mom." I gulped down another sob.

Mom's expression softened, and she put her arms around me. "Honey, I don't know what's happening here, but I know that Shari is a wonderful young woman, and we are lucky to have her—"

"Mm-hm. I know." I nodded.

"And we're all grateful to you for bringing her into the family." Mom wiped my tears, just as she had done when I was little. "I think we were all blessed when the Lord let your old clunker die." She smiled.

I burst into tears again.

"Look, honey, I don't know what's going on with you and Shari, or why you feel so startled by this news. Most of us have seen it coming for weeks."

"Yeah. Apparently." I failed to keep the sarcasm out of my voice.

Mom frowned. "This little drama is making the whole family uneasy." She lifted my chin with her finger. "Dry your tears, wash your face, then come out and congratulate them both." She didn't add, "Do you understand?" but she didn't have to. "Don't be too long," she said, closing the door behind her.

I drew in a few long, shaky breaths, and then dutifully dried my tears and washed my face. When I thought I could make it through the necessary speeches without further embarrassment, I straightened my clothing, took one more deep breath, and paced back down the hall.

I found Noah in the kitchen, helping Wendy and Denise load the dishwasher while Josh and his wife, Barbara, washed pots and pans. Shari was nowhere to be seen. That would make this part easier. "Noah," I said as I approached him, "can I have a hug?"

"Sure, sis." Noah's tone was noncommittal, but he put both arms around me and gave me a good, strong squeeze.

"I'm so happy for you both," I said. He might have found it easier to believe me if my eyes hadn't been tearing up again. "I . . . I'm sorry about earlier."

"I believe you," he said, and I think he did—now, anyway. "But you and Shari will need to talk. She's pretty upset."

"I know." I looked around. "Where is she?"

"She took Kerry to the bathroom. She'd like to have her fully accident-proof before the wedding."

"And when will that be?"

"There's some paperwork to clear up," he said, and I realized he meant having Shari's earlier sealing canceled. "We're hoping for the last Saturday in April, right after Shari graduates."

"That sounds great," I told him. "So what can I do to help here?"

I pitched in and helped in the kitchen for awhile, hoping Shari would come back, but when the kitchen was cleaned and in order and she still hadn't returned, I decided it might be better if we talked later, away from the rest of the family. I gave my thanks to Mom and Dad, my hugs and good-byes to everyone else, and headed back across the valley.

At home that evening, I busied myself with preparing the clothing I'd wear to school the next day and writing a long, tearful entry in my journal, but Shari and Kerry still hadn't come home by the time I'd finished. With my journal in my lap, I found myself reading back, beginning with the happy entries from Valentine's Day a year ago, then working my way slowly through the record of my heartbreak. Kyle's revelation—and the end of my engagement—had come just nine days after Valentine's Day, shortly before the end of February.

It shocked me to see the anger and betrayal practically boiling off those pages. In the midst of my hurt and pain, I had never realized how bitter or how just plain selfish I had been—indifferent to the pain of others except where it gave me an appeal to their sympathy. It was a testament to my family's love that they'd been willing to put up with me at all.

Then a thought struck with hurricane force. Was that why I'd failed to notice what was growing between Noah and Shari? I knew I'd grown a lot since my experience with Kyle—so much of the rage and hurt I saw reflected in the pages of my journal had been softened and washed away through the healing power of the Atonement in the past few months. But I knew that some of the walls I had built were still in the process of coming down. Had Shari and Noah chosen not to share their growing feelings for one another simply because I'd been so wrapped up in myself, so unapproachable? Even the possibility made me want to cringe. Maybe they didn't owe me an apology after all. Maybe I owed them one—a large one.

Steeling myself to the idea of eating crow as soon as I saw Shari again, I prepared myself for bed and then dressed in my warmest, snuggly jammies. I cuddled up in my big easy chair with my journal and continued reading through old entries and marveling at the Lord's intervention in my life.

It was well after midnight when I awoke, shivering, in my easy chair. The front porch light had been turned off, and a quick look inside the garage let me know that Harry had been fed. Sometime in the past couple of hours, Shari had tiptoed in, put Kerry to bed, and gone about her evening routine without waking me. She was now secluded in the room she shared with her daughter. There would be no crow-eating tonight.

Chapter 13

Shari and Kerry were already gone by the time I got up the next morning, postponing even further the opportunity to put things right. By now I was finally grasping the idea that the wish which had been so close to my heart only days earlier was actually coming true: Shari and her sweet baby girl were going to be part of my family. If there had been some lack of communication in how it all came about, well, that wasn't such a big problem, was it? Surely we could get past all this if I could just find some time to talk with Shari. That she was deliberately avoiding me was becoming more than obvious.

I thought about Noah and Shari all morning. I kept running scripts in my mind, rehearsing what I'd say to her. Though I tried to put those thoughts on the back burner to give my class my full attention, I found that they kept jumping into the foreground. My preoccupation quickly became apparent to my third graders. Sweet kids one and all, they rarely fail to take advantage whenever they see potential weakness in the adult defenses. By lunchtime I had half a dozen names on the Behavior Blackboard.

I didn't have lunch duty that week, so I took my brown bag into the teachers' lounge and tried to relax by listening to the buzz around the room, but my need to talk to Shari was growing. I hadn't even finished my carrot sticks before I put down my lunch and walked to the office to use the staff phone. I dialed her cell phone, turned my back to the secretary in the corner, and waited for Shari to answer. When I got her voice mail, I disconnected. What I had to say couldn't be left in a message. I tried twice more before lunch was over and got voice mail both times. Finally I left a message that said I hoped we could talk soon. That was the best I could do.

It helped, too. The afternoon went a little better than the morning. I found I was more focused and more mentally available to the kids when they needed me. It also helped that Miss Despain took them all in midafternoon for their monthly environmental science lesson. I called Shari twice more and got voice mail both times, then spent the rest of my free time catching up on grading math papers. At the end of the day, I welcomed back my kids, who taught me a few new facts about the trees on our school campus. By the closing bell I decided my teaching day hadn't been wasted after all.

I quickly tidied up the classroom and headed for home a bit earlier than usual, but it was with major anxiety that I turned onto my street. The tension between Shari and me had proven to me just how important my roommate had become in my life. I knew now how grateful I'd be to have her as a sister and Kerry as my niece. I also knew that the coming conversation would not be easy, but I wanted to get on with it. I was still running scripts in my head.

When I pulled into the garage, I was surprised to find Shari's car already there. She was waiting for me in the kitchen, so she got the opening line. I guessed she had done some scripting of her own.

"Hi," she said, a bit stiffly. "I left Kerry at my mom's, and dinner's in the oven. I think we need to talk."

"I agree," I said. "Can we start with a hug?"

She hesitated only briefly, but I could see the tension relax a bit as she said, "Sure," and stepped toward me.

I held her a long time and squeezed hard. I wanted my hug to say *I love you, and I want you as my sister. Welcome to the family.* I hoped it did.

"Now sit," she said, and sat down at the dining table. I joined her. "I—"

"Wait. Let me start," I said.

Shari nodded.

"I need to apologize," I told her and saw her defenses come down a little. "I know I've been preoccupied with my own pain and worries. I hadn't realized it, but I know I must have been fairly unavailable to you—emotionally, that is." Shari looked uncertain about how to respond, so I plunged on. "I felt so hurt when I realized you and Noah had been developing this kind of close relationship right under my nose, and I didn't know a thing about it, but—"

"The question is," Shari said quietly, "why didn't you know?"

I felt my brow furrow. Wasn't that perfectly obvious? "I didn't know because you didn't say anything."

"Should we have had to?" Shari was giving me a very pointed, searching look. "Others saw what was happening. Why didn't you?"

"I thought we were close," I said, trying to keep the pain out of my voice. "I thought for sure you'd talk to me. I mean, here I had almost begun to think of you and Kerry as family, and I thought—"

"Almost," Shari repeated, interrupting me.

"What?"

"You said you had *almost* begun to think of us as family."

I just stared at her. "What are you talking about?"

Shari sighed. "Noah wanted to tell you some time ago, Sarah. I asked him not to."

"Why not?"

"Because of your obvious disapproval."

"What?" I jumped to my feet. "Disapproval? Shari, I—"

"You thought I was good enough to be your roommate," Shari said, her voice tight, "but I wasn't good enough for Noah. You could *'almost'* see me as family, as a comfortable hanger-on at Kimball gatherings maybe, but when it came right down to it, you couldn't see a woman with a divorce and a child behind her as being worthy of your brother."

"Oh, Shari, no! It's nothing like that!" I was still standing.

Shari stood to join me. "Isn't it? Then why did it never occur to you that Noah might be interested?"

"I—" I felt dumbfounded. "I don't know. I guess I just thought that one of you would talk to me. But disapproval? Never! I was just thinking a few days ago how I wished you and Kerry were actually a part of my family."

"If that's true," Shari said, "why didn't it occur to you that there was a way to make it happen? Why didn't you notice how much time I was spending with Noah?"

"I knew you were gone a lot, but—"

"Oh, come on, Sarah. We were together at every family dinner. He often helped me put Kerry to bed when we brought her home. Everyone in your family noticed our interest in each other but you— and you live right here! If you can't be honest with yourself, at least be honest with me."

"That's not fair! I *am* being honest!" But even as I said it, a cold shiver ran down my spine, and I found myself wondering if it was true.

Shari sighed. I could see her running through all the scripts she had been rehearsing. I'd have done the same if any of my scripts had prepared me for this, but I'd been out of my depth since her first sentence.

"Look," she said finally, "It's been obvious for awhile that you don't approve of divorces or divorced people. I can only assume that you think Noah deserves something better than to 'buy into someone else's problems.'"

"Shari, that's not—"

She stopped me with a look, an expression so sad and hurt it shocked me. "I think I'd better go pick up Kerry," she said, and started toward the door. "I'll probably be late."

"I—I don't know what to say," I stammered.

"Whatever else happens, I want you to know how grateful I am that you brought me into your home and introduced me to your family. I love Noah. I *love* him, Sarah. So does Kerry. We've prayed about becoming an eternal family, and we believe the Lord has confirmed our decision. I'd like to think that both you and your family will accept us, but whether you ever do or not, I thank you for what you've done." She opened the door to the garage.

"Please don't go." My tears were flowing freely.

"I'll be late," she said, her eyes down, then she closed the door behind her.

I watched her go, feeling helpless and befuddled and terribly misunderstood. How could she have thought . . . ?

I stood there for a long time, just looking at the closed garage door. At last, I sank into the chair. My mind went back to the conclusion I had come to the night before: I had been self-absorbed and preoccupied with my own worries. It wasn't nice, but it was true. But could there be more going on? Trying to be honest with myself, I began to ponder what I might have said or done to make Shari feel I disapproved. Was she just being oversensitive? I shook my head. If that were the case, surely Noah would have said something. He had gone along with keeping their secret. Did he agree with Shari's conclusion?

After awhile I realized the sun was down and I was going to have to start turning on lights. I took Shari's dinner out of the oven—a delicious chicken casserole that was one of my favorites from Shari's repertoire—and got out a plate. I said a long, thoughtful prayer over the food, asking for enlightenment so I might understand how I had hurt these lovely people who meant so much to me. Then I ate my dinner, barely noticing the hearty flavors I usually loved, while I pondered further, replaying different scenes over and over in my mind.

Was it possible that Shari was right? I dropped my fork halfway to my mouth. Surely I didn't really disapprove of Shari. But a funny feeling began curdling in my stomach as I remembered something she had said: *If it's true that you wanted me in your family, why didn't you see that there was a way to make it happen?*

Images began to parade through my mind: Deb and Brian posing outside the Salt Lake Temple when I was twelve years old; Josh and Barbara coming out of the Bountiful Temple when I was fourteen; Tim and Wendy at Mount Timpanogos five years ago; Seth and Denise at Jordan River just four months later. These were my models for how eternal marriage looked in my family. Shari was right about one thing: There weren't any three-year-olds or lurking ex-spouses in any of those pictures. Was it possible that I hadn't seen what was right under my nose because I didn't expect Noah's eternal companion to have a marital history? I had just stood up to clear the table and put the leftover casserole away, and I suddenly had to sit down again. Was it possible that somewhere, deep down inside, I held a negative judgment of divorced single mothers?

I said the words aloud—"divorced single mother"—and the thoughts that popped into my head weren't kind. Maybe I had shown Shari a prejudice I had been sheltering unconsciously. I heard my own voice arguing, "But Shari isn't like that!" And that was when another voice, one I often attributed to the Spirit, whispered, "Maybe very few LDS single mothers are *like that*."

Ouch.

I thought of Aunt Lizbeth and used cars. I thought of Ruth saying that I might be ruling out some great guys when I told her I didn't want to be set up with anyone who'd been divorced. I cringed as I remembered my reply: "Why buy someone else's problems?"

My usual bedtime found me on my knees again, praying for forgiveness and for another sweet change of heart. It took some time, but at last peace came, and with it a new resolve to make things right.

I began running new mental scripts for my next chat with Shari. I also resolved to take a new look at the divorced singles I knew, and become more open to including them among my friends. Then, planning to catch Shari when she came home, I sat down in my easy chair with my journal and my scriptures, wrote a long journal entry, and continued my preparation for my Relief Society lesson that Sunday which—wouldn't you know it?—was called "Forgiving Others with All of Our Hearts."

With Harry purring beside me, I read of the Savior's mercy and love for everyone He encountered. After a moment I closed my eyes, offering a fervent prayer that the last vestiges of anger I had harbored toward Kyle and his wife might be washed away, that my heart would be cleansed of all unkind thoughts and bitterness toward others, and that I could let go of unrighteous judgments of anyone—particularly of sweet souls like Shari and Kerry, who had not been guilty of any wrongdoing but had been victimized by the sins of another. This time the peace that washed through me was thorough, welcome, and sweet. It came with such complete relief that I wasn't even anxious about talking to Shari when I saw her next.

It wasn't long before she came in, Noah behind her with a sleeping Kerry in his arms. I ran to meet them, throwing my arms around Shari. "I'm so sorry, sis," I said, whispering to avoid waking Kerry. "Welcome to the family."

She slowly returned my hug. "Are you sure—"

"You're right that I should have noticed, but I want you to know that I love you, and I'm so glad you're going to be a Kimball now." I held her away and beamed at her.

"Do you really mean that?" she asked.

"With all my heart," I said, realizing I had just used the title of Sunday's lesson. "Please forgive me for making you feel unwanted, and know that I'm here for you. Anything I can do to help, just ask."

I gave Shari another quick hug and stood on my tiptoes to plant a quick kiss on Noah's cheek. "Congratulations, LostArkGuy."

He grinned, looking as though I'd relieved him of a heavy burden. Kerry stirred in his arms and he whispered, "I think I'd better go put our little girl to bed." Shari nodded, and Noah started down the hall.

"So you're sure you're okay with this?" Shari asked, her expression hopeful.

"Much more than okay," I assured her.

Shari dropped her gaze for a moment, and I could tell she was gearing up to say something uncomfortable. "Listen, Sarah, I need to—"

"I'll understand if it takes you awhile to feel comfortable with me—"

"No!" She caught my hand. "Sarah, I need to apologize, too."

"No, Shari, really—"

She quieted me with a look, then her eyes twinkled as she said, "Okay, I *really* need to apologize."

The tension between us broke as I smiled, too.

"Look," she began, "I was awfully harsh with you today—"

"I deserved it."

"No, never like that. We've been too close—at least most of the time." She paused. "You're right on the other point, too. I could have said something. I should have. You gave me plenty of opportunities. And I could have let Noah tell you. I guess I was just feeling sensitive. Maybe I was even afraid that I *wasn't* worthy of him—you know, the 'used goods' syndrome."

"Oh, Shari! No!"

"It's okay. Noah knew how I was feeling. When I went to him tonight, all teary and stressed, he suggested we go to see my bishop. I'm glad we did—he's a wonderful bishop."

I nodded and squeezed her hand.

"He talked with us both for awhile, and then he asked if I would like a blessing. I think it was the most beautiful blessing I've ever been given. I know now that the Lord approves of me."

I smiled and wiped a tear that had trickled down my cheek.

"The Lord approves of me, Noah approves of me, and now I know *you* approve of me."

"I'm your biggest fan."

"Then maybe I can approve of me, too." She smiled and hugged me again.

As she stepped away, I said, "You were right about me too, you know. I mean, you were right about my harboring some prejudices. I just hadn't recognized . . ."

"I know, Sarah. I heard you when you were talking to Ruth."

"Huh?"

"When she was signing you up for that computer dating service and you said you wouldn't go out with anyone who'd been divorced. You said—"

"I said, 'Why buy someone else's problems?' Oh, Shari, you weren't supposed to hear that."

"I know I wasn't. But I did hear you, Sarah, and I knew what it meant. That was when I told Noah I didn't want him to say anything."

"I'm so sorry I hurt you," I replied in a quavering voice.

"It's okay. It doesn't matter anymore—not if you've decided you're really okay with me marrying into your family."

"I'm so much more than okay with it. I love you, Shari." We were both crying by the time we hugged again.

Noah came in from the hallway. "My turn to get in on all this hugging," he said, and the three of us—Shari, Noah, and I—had one big group hug in the kitchen. Then we stayed up much later than we should have, talking about how they hoped to be married in the Jordan River Temple in a couple of months and batting around ideas for their reception. When Shari asked if I'd be her maid of honor, I was delighted to accept.

* * *

On Friday, I left for school feeling like I could take on the world—which, interestingly enough, was what I wound up doing. Our weather had warmed up a bit as it often does in February—a bit of false spring before the tail end of winter whips us—so I had my class out on the playground doing kickball relays when Mr. Salazar approached me with a proposition.

"I've just been talking with the president of our PTO," he said as he joined me. "The organization has some funding earmarked for repainting our ball courts. With the success of your Project Valentine, they've been talking about adding in a large, scaled map of the world. I'd like your class to paint it."

"Wow," I responded, feeling both elation and hesitance. "I'm not much of an artist, though, and my third graders can spread paint, but—"

"Mrs. Jeffers says she'll borrow the pattern for a similar map at her son's middle school and then chalk it in for you. Then your kids can paint each of the continents in a different color."

"How big a map are we talking about?"

"Pretty big. Probably twenty-five feet by forty or so."

"Wow," I said again, then nodded. "I think we can do that."

"The kicker is, they'll want you to mark the rough location of our school on the North American map and the general location of the Project Valentine soldiers on the opposite side of the globe. They'd also like to see you paint the silhouette of a third-grade boy and girl on our side and the silhouette of a soldier in uniform on the other. Mr. Pastori has agreed to be the model for the soldier, and his class is researching army uniforms so they can paint in the details. Your class will paint the map and the third graders. Does that sound workable to you?"

"It sounds great." I was already imagining the geography lessons I could work into the project. "How soon would you like us to start?"

"Mrs. Jeffers says she'll borrow the pattern over the weekend and trace it out for you in the evenings next week. If you'll buy the paint sometime over the next few days, say by next weekend, the PTO will reimburse you and you can start any time after that."

"Perfect," I answered, anticipating my next visit to the art supply store.

As it turned out, Mrs. Jeffers' part of the project took longer than she expected—she drew a *very* exact map of the continents—so it was the next weekend before I made my trip to the art supply store. The week in between was spent making up for lost time with Shari and Noah, sometimes watching Kerry while they were out together and sometimes going with them to look at cakes or cultural halls where they might have their reception.

Although Shari said she had already had one big party and didn't need another, she wanted everything to be beautiful for Noah and for Kerry, who was possibly just old enough to remember this experience as her first model of a wedding. For his part, Noah insisted that Shari deserved a beautiful reception. He said he would like to keep things simple but elegant, and Shari heartily agreed, although she seemed unsure about the specifics. I assured her I'd be available whenever she needed me.

* * *

That Saturday, Ruth came over to help me paint the living room—I had chosen Sweet Desert Sage, a lovely gray-green that went well with my old furniture. Ruth also stayed over to help with my lesson on Sunday. The sisters were generous and helpful as always, and I came away with an even deeper understanding of the principle of forgiveness and a greater appreciation of the sacred power of the Atonement. By the time I slept that Sunday, I could honestly say I bore no ill will toward either Kyle or his wife, or even the sad, confused man who had hurt Shari and Kerry so badly and had lost his eternal family in the process. His loss was our family's gain.

On Thursday evening, Noah took Shari and Kerry to a family movie, and I sat down with my journal. The following day would mark a full year since my breakup with Kyle, but I no longer felt like rehashing old news. Instead, I started a new entry, writing about how happy I was that Shari would be joining the Kimball clan.

As I prepared for bed that evening, I realized I was happy—really happy. I was feeling fairly good about myself, too. My confidence had been renewed since my forgiveness had become real, and I realized that this must be the reason we were commanded to forgive others. The act had not only cleansed my own heart and restored my faith in others, but it had boosted my faith in myself. Again I marveled at the Lord's wisdom.

As I drifted off to sleep, I thought of Justin Owen and his gift in pushing me toward forgiveness and greater charity. I wondered where he was and what he was doing and whether he might be interested in giving our relationship another chance now that I was no longer obsessed with my old wounds. I decided that the next day, if I felt brave enough, I might even give him a call. Why not?

Throughout the following day, I mentally rehearsed what I would say to Justin. I'd thank him again for the book he had given me and tell him how much I had learned and how grateful I was for the painful but enlightening lesson. I'd ask how he was doing and make polite conversation, giving him the option of picking up where we had left off if he felt like doing so. If he didn't, well, I didn't have anything to lose by thanking him, did I?

I was humming and happy as I drove home that evening. I still had Justin's cell number, and I felt confident and relaxed about the call I planned to make as soon as I walked through the door. I stopped to pick up the mail before going in and saw that there was a formal white envelope with my name and address handwritten on the front in my mailbox. Although I didn't recognize the return address, I eagerly opened the invitation, wondering who was getting married.

Mr. and Mrs. Delmar Lytle
are pleased to announce
the marriage of their daughter
Stephanie Jean
to
Justin Harley Owen
son of Patrick and Cheryl Owen
on Friday, the sixteenth day of March,
in the Provo Temple . . .

The rest of the words blurred before my eyes, and I had to pause to catch my breath. It wasn't like I'd been counting on anything happening with Justin. I had given up on that two months earlier, but the news still stung, and I couldn't quite quash out the snide voice reminding me that within one calendar year, two men had left me for other women. I allowed myself a small pity party and a pint of Ben and Jerry's.

Chapter 14

Saturday dawned bright and clear and beautiful. My small emotional storm of the night before had passed, and my attitude was cheerier. Noah and Shari were taking Kerry with them on a picnic drive up the Alpine Loop, and my plans with Ruth to paint "her" bedroom and then take her shopping for her birthday had fallen through due to some major activity in Helaman Halls, so I spent the morning catching up on laundry and other domestic chores.

A little before noon, I screwed together my courage and called Justin, congratulated him on his forthcoming marriage, and thanked him again for his thoughtful gift. He was a bit tentative, but I was able to tell him I was glad for him—and mean it—and he relaxed.

We ended up chatting like old friends, which in a way I guess we were. Just days after we had parted, he had bumped into a girl he'd dated when they were both high school students in Florida. They'd lost touch when her family had moved to Minnesota while he was away at the Y, and although he'd tried to find her a few times, they hadn't seen each other again until that memorable new beginning. With a long, solid past to build on, their relationship had progressed rapidly. He assured me they were very happy together and very well suited, and that it was destiny that had brought them together again. I offered my heartfelt best wishes.

That phone call ended any lingering feelings of self-pity over Justin, and I realized that he had been the last loose end I needed to tie up in order to put the past year of difficult growth behind me. I took a partly-symbolic shower and emerged feeling fresh and new, ready to face my future. As I touched up my face in the mirror, I told myself this moment was the beginning of the rest of my life. It was clichéd and cheesy, but it made me feel good, and I was humming when I left home.

I had planned a series of errands starting with bringing some lightly-used baby clothes a friend had given me up to Deb and working my way back across the valley. I'd pick up a birthday present for Ruth, who was turning nineteen on the coming Monday, stop at Allie's, my now-favorite art supply store, and then shop for groceries just before returning.

My visit with Deb went longer than I'd planned, though I should have known to allow for more time since I almost always spent longer than I expected when I visited with the family's new babies. Lauren was just getting to that adorable stage where she could recognize and smile at people, and I spent a pleasurable couple of hours bouncing her and cooing at her until Deb put her down for a nap. Then, since Brian was out with his elders quorum helping a family move and Lauren wasn't sleeping through the night yet, I read stories to the older kids for another hour so Deb could nap, too.

The visit at Deb's reminded me of how Ruth had complimented the gift blanket I'd made for Lauren and how she said she'd love to learn to knit someday. When Brian returned home, I drove to the strip mall, parked near Allie's Art Mart, and then went straight to the sewing-and-homecrafts department of the big box store across the parking lot, trying to find the perfect how-to book plus appropriate needles and yarn as my gift for Ruth. I spent some time wandering up and down the aisles, but I couldn't find anything that looked like my baby sister.

Thanks to the little bulge in my budget, I was able to think about what I'd like to give her rather than what I could afford, which was a big confidence booster; however, I was discovering that it also took more time to browse for the perfect gift than to settle for what would work. As I thought more of the kind of person Ruth was, I concluded that just because she'd said she would love to learn *someday* didn't mean she wanted to start knitting *now*. Frustrated, I moved to the stationery section, where I found a cute card, but I left without a gift.

The light was just fading as I stepped outside. Streetlights were blinking on everywhere, and I took a quick look across the parking lot, hoping the Art Mart stayed open late on Saturdays.

It did. There were still lights on inside, and people were going in and out. I sighed with relief as I started across the lot. Just then something caught my eye, and I turned to notice the banner in the LDS bookstore just down the way from Allie's, apparently advertising some new book they were premiering. I couldn't read the title, but it occurred to me that, if the book was new, it might be something Ruth hadn't read yet—a feat in itself, since Ruth devoured books almost as avidly as Ellen Brenner did. I made sure that Allie's would be open for a little while longer, then began walking toward the bookstore.

As I turned the corner toward the bookstore, a familiar image came into view. With a chill, I did a double-take. My eyes weren't playing tricks on me—*Embrace* was the cover art for the new premiere book, *In His Arms: Sacred Works* by Craig Emory. I half ran through the front doors, picked up the book from the central display, and began turning through it, oblivious to the passing time as I admired one beautiful, touching portrayal of the Savior after another, interspersed with the artist's comments.

The center foldout was a double spread of *Embrace,* with the painting on the left, and a close-up detail of the Savior with outstretched arms on the right. Beside it were the artist's words:

> This is one of my favorite pieces. I worked on it during a critical period when I was facing deep personal challenges and felt particular need of the Lord's Atonement. I hoped to capture how He feels toward each of us and the love He must feel in taking each of our individual burdens upon Himself. I also wanted to show the gratitude of the penitent and forgiven sinner—my own personal gratitude for His love and mercy and the effects of the Atonement in my life.

I was blinking back tears as I reverently closed the book and placed it in my shopping cart. The artist's words had captured my feelings with almost the same power as his images, and it touched me that he had created the painting out of specific, personal need.

Embrace had certainly filled that role for me, and probably for others as well. Thinking gratefully of my Barbie dollars, I added a second copy of the book to my cart. The first was for Ruth; the second was all mine.

I was just becoming aware of time and place again when I remembered I had another stop to make before closing time, so I hurried through checkout and back to the Art Mart. I chose not to waste time by looking up and down the aisles, but went straight to their customer service desk, where I was lucky to find Allison herself, along with the young clerk who had helped to arrange the school discount last time. The owner greeted me like an old friend. "Good evening, Miss Kimball, and congratulations. I saw the article on your project in the *Deseret News*."

"That was a surprise," I told her, "but a nice one."

"It was very nice," she agreed. "Thanks for mentioning our store. We've had a lot of comments on the story."

"It was the least I could do. You were a big help. Hey, I'm working on a new project, and I need some outdoor paints. Can you tell me where I might find them?"

"Those will be on 14B," Allison said. "Is this for the school again?"

I described what we were doing, and she said, "Be sure to ask for the educational discount at the register."

I thanked her again and breezed down to 14B with a grin on my face. The aisle held an astonishing array of paints, and I was still studying the shelves when a warm voice behind me said, "Miss Kimball?"

I turned. "Yes?"

The man standing behind me was a little taller than Noah, though probably somewhat older. I was immediately attracted to his gentle smile and clear, blue eyes. "I just wanted to congratulate you," he said. "It seems I'm a fan of your work."

"*My* work?"

He nodded. "I saw the stories on your Project Valentine. I think that was great what you did for the soldiers, and I always like it when kids use their art in meaningful ways."

"But how did you know—"

"I spoke to Allison when I came in. When I congratulated her on her store's mention in the *Deseret News,* she told me the teacher who led the project had just walked down aisle fourteen. I'm glad I caught you."

"Then I'm glad, too," I said. "Mr. . . . ?"

"I'm sorry, I should have introduced myself. It's Emory, Craig Emory."

I caught my breath and felt my eyes widen. "Craig Emory the artist?"

He smiled. "You know my work?"

I opened the bookstore bag I'd brought inside with me and showed him my purchases. "It seems I'm a fan of your work, too."

"Two copies?" he asked.

"One is a gift, and the other is for me." Then I took a deep breath. "Since you're here, maybe I can ask you to sign them for me?"

"Um, yeah, of course. Happy to." He fumbled for a pen. I handed him one, and he used my shopping cart as a base while he asked me what I'd like him to write in Ruth's book. I settled for "Happy Birthday, Ruth."

In the second book, he wrote, "Good to meet you, Sarah," and signed his name.

He handed the books back to me, and for a long, awkward moment we just stood there looking at each other, silly grins on our faces. The spell was broken when the intercom came on, advising customers that the store would be closing in fifteen minutes.

"I don't want to hold you up," he began.

"I won't be long," I said. "I just have to pick up some outdoor paints for another project at the school. We're painting a map of the world."

"Here. These are the paints you need," he said, pointing them out. Then, as I picked out my colors, he asked, "What kind of map? How large? How detailed?" Over the next few minutes, we chatted as comfortably as if we were dear friends as I finished my selections and he gathered several tubes of oils and acrylics. We checked out side by side, the last two customers in the store, and wandered out together.

Then we just kept talking. He walked with me while I put the paint in the trunk of my car, and I walked with him, still telling him about the genesis of Project Valentine, while he put his paints into the passenger seat of his pickup truck. It seemed like the most natural thing in the world when he looked up, spotted the open sign on a small restaurant and asked, "Do you like Thai?"

"Love it," I answered, and we continued our talk about his work and mine over pad Thai noodles, steamed snow peas, and delicious ginger pork.

I told him about the recent successes of Henry Jackson and Bao Vang, described the current uneasy peace between Ellen and Lillian Brenner, and shared my excitement over the upcoming effort to memorialize Project Valentine on the blacktop near our ball courts. He shared his excitement about when his first painting sold, then described his lean years as a struggling artist, selling a painting here, accepting a small commission there, and doing odd jobs to make ends meet while he completed his MFA. He said he had never intended to sell *Embrace* but had been so desperate for cash that the offer seemed more than he could refuse. Later, when his art had become successful enough to provide a good living, he had looked up the purchaser and bought the painting back. "I have it hanging in my living room," he said. "If I can help it, I won't ever let it go again."

My voice was choked with emotion as I told him about my first experience with *Embrace* during his MFA show and related what his painting had come to mean to me.

"You picture it when you pray?" he said, sounding awestruck.

"It has always helped me to visualize a loving and accepting Savior."

"Oh. Wow." He looked pensive. "I know what my work means to me, but I don't believe I've ever met anyone who saw it the same way. My wife never—"

I froze. "You have a wife?" I looked around uncomfortably. Was I really having dinner with a married man?

"I'm sorry. I should have said ex-wife." As he spoke, he briefly touched my hand—a quick, reassuring gesture. "It's been nearly three years since the divorce, but I still slip sometimes. As much as I've enjoyed your company, please know that I wouldn't be here, having dinner with you, if I were still a married man."

"I'm glad to hear that," I said with obvious relief. Then I added, "You know, this isn't the sort of thing I would normally do—having dinner with a stranger, I mean."

He sat back, looking thoughtful. "I guess I haven't been thinking of it that way. I was so impressed with the work you were doing with your school kids that I almost felt I knew you. I don't feel like I've been talking with a stranger."

"I haven't really felt that, either," I admitted. "I know your work so well I can't help feeling I know the artist, too."

His voice was low and full of meaning when he said, "In some important ways, I think you do."

For a moment we sat, focusing on one another. Then I asked, "So, do you want to talk about it?"

He looked confused. "The painting?"

"The divorce."

He shrugged, looking away. "Not much to tell, and it doesn't make very nice dinner conversation."

"I'll tell my heartbreak story if you tell yours," I said, deliberately keeping it light.

He looked surprised. "You're divorced, too?"

"No, nothing that dramatic. I was engaged to a man who left me to marry another woman. It wasn't quite a left-at-the-altar situation, but we were down to just six weeks." I shrugged. "Not much else to say, really." And I was surprised to realize there wasn't.

"Still painful, I'd guess," he said, his voice full of sympathy.

"It was rough going for awhile, but I think my pride was hurt much worse than my heart. I'm past it now."

"How long ago did it happen?"

"Just more than a year. You said that it's been three years for you, right?"

"Right," he answered. "That is, three years since the divorce was final." He didn't go on.

"Your turn," I prompted.

He smiled. "I know. I'm just trying to decide how much to tell, and how far back to start. Are you sure you want to hear this?"

"It's up to you, but I'll listen if you're willing to share."

He looked sheepish. "This isn't exactly the sort of thing people usually talk about when they first meet . . ."

I smiled, feeling bold. "I think we agreed this hasn't been a usual first meeting."

He nodded. "No, it hasn't. You're right about that." Then slowly he began. "I met Lisa about a year after my mission."

"Where did you serve?"

"Bolivia—the top of the world. Loved it, but that's another story."

I waited, playing with my snow peas.

"Lisa was a business and finance major, and I was taking a double major in business and art. We dated for nearly a year before I proposed. I made no secret of my intention to pursue the master's degree in art and to use my practical training to support my art business—writing bids and business plans, that kind of stuff—but Lisa saw business as my real work and art as my hobby. She always thought I'd come around and see reason."

He shook his head, and I could see he was struggling a bit with the next part. "I started the graduate degree about the time Lisa decided it was time for her to quit work so we could start a family. By then my art was beginning to show success. I had always believed the Lord meant for me to paint, and I didn't want to give it up without a fair try."

"That seems reasonable."

He shook his head. "Lisa didn't think so. She kept saying that she hadn't married a starving artist and didn't want to live like one. We tried to make it work between us for awhile, but she was so unhappy. I begged her to give it a little longer, but she insisted I get a job. So I did."

"You did?" I hadn't expected that turn in the story.

"I did. I put the paints in the garage, put on my suit, and landed a management job in a big retail store. I got my first paycheck and my first major art commission on the same day. The next day I was served with divorce papers."

"Oh, Craig! The commission wasn't enough to bring her back?"

He shook his head. "By then there was another man in the picture, and she was eager to finalize things."

"I'm so sorry." I had some idea of how much that must have hurt.

There was a long, awkward pause, and then he said, "I found out later that he'd been around for awhile. He and Lisa had known each other when they were kids in southern Utah. They'd dated in high school before he went on his mission, then broke up before he left." He paused again. "Are you sure you want to hear this?"

"Only if you want to tell me."

He shook his head. "This is crazy," he said, but I gave him an encouraging smile and he went on. "After Lisa and I were married, he showed up again, working where she worked, and I guess things just went from there." He shrugged. "But I'm talking too much."

I laid my hand over his. "No, you're not. Not at all." I paused. "That other man . . . Didn't he realize Lisa was married?"

"He was married, too."

I shook my head. "I'm so sorry." Then suddenly I understood. "That was when you painted *Embrace,* wasn't it?"

He looked at me intently. "How did you know?"

I shrugged. "I just knew. You were working through your feelings about Lisa, the other man, and the divorce, and . . ." I hesitated to say it. "And your own worthiness."

"That's . . . remarkably insightful." He gave me an odd, wary look. "It's a little scary, really—like you're reading my mind."

Again I shrugged. "I've been there." The realization of how similar our experiences must have been struck me forcefully. His experience was like mine, like Shari's. I suddenly thought of Kerry. "You didn't have children?"

"No, thank goodness. I'd have hated for a child to be involved. There weren't any children in the other man's marriage, either."

"That's a blessing." I told him about Shari and her daughter, and how Shari had come to live in my house and was now engaged to my brother. "She's had a rough go of it, but she's doing well now," I concluded.

"It sounds like her story has a happy ending," he said wistfully.

A few moments later, our server arrived to ask if we'd like dessert, then packaged up our leftovers when we both declined. Craig grabbed the bill, and when I volunteered to pay for my dinner (this wasn't a date, after all—or was it?), he simply smiled and replied, "My treat," and handed our server a debit card.

"Tell me more about your commissions," I said as the server left. "Who hires you? What kinds of work?"

I learned that Craig collected RFPs, or requests for proposals, from various public agencies interested in art projects and then submitted proposals with sketches of the work he planned. He was also hired on occasion by individuals who wanted a specific size of canvas for their homes or business places and who liked his style. Not all of it was religious art, either. He had paintings of various secular subjects in a number of public buildings in and around the Salt Lake Valley, and a couple of one-man shows scheduled over the coming months. The more he talked, the more impressed I became. I knew there were many aspiring artists but few who were able to make art a paying career. Yet Craig seemed to be doing well. My mind was forming an image of the shadowy figure of Lisa, and I wondered if she ever regretted her choice.

In no time at all, the server came to the table to announce, "We close at ten-thirty."

"Oh, sorry," Craig said.

I looked at my watch. "It can't be that late already, can it?"

"I'm afraid so," he answered. Then he stood and helped me with my jacket. "I'll walk you to your car."

Although the night air was turning crisp, we talked at my car for another forty-five minutes before we finally used his offer to help with the world map as an excuse to exchange phone numbers and e-mail addresses.

It was nearing midnight as I pulled up to the grocery store, hours later than I'd expected to be there. I was grateful I had a list with me as I zoomed through the store that Saturday evening, trying to keep to the letter of the law as well as the spirit.

I hustled home and found Shari's car in the garage and my roommates already sleeping. I had expected that—Noah and Shari had set a fairly strict curfew for themselves to avoid spending late hours alone together—but I was still disappointed. I would have loved to share my evening's experience.

Humming softly, I put my groceries away and prepared the few things I'd need for the morning. Then, unable to help myself, I checked my e-mail. Though there was nothing from Craig yet, there was a message from Mormons2Marry.com, an announcement that the company was going out of business. I tried not to smile too widely as I read that those who were still owed introductions should plan to use them up before the end of March. Shaking my head, I moved my cursor to close down my e-mail. Just then a new message popped up:

```
Hello again, Sarah. Just a quick note
to tell you how much I enjoyed this
evening. I'm looking forward to stop-
ping by the school on Monday afternoon.
I'll register at the office then meet
you at the ball fields. Have a great
Sunday, and I'll see you soon, Craig.
```

I shivered with excitement and anticipation and then typed back a simple message:

```
Looking forward to it. I had a great
time, too, Sarah.
```

As I reached for the SEND button, I realized that Craig would know I'd been up at twelve forty-five looking for his e-mail, and I wondered if it was wise to violate my mother's dating advice never to look too eager. Then I hit the button anyway. I didn't care if he knew I was interested. I was.

As I prepared for sleep, I paused for a long look in the mirror. It humbled me to recognize that I very much wanted to spend more time with Craig, yet I never would have considered dating him if I hadn't met him first. I hadn't asked how old he was, but I was fairly certain he was more than four years older, and I knew he was divorced. If he had been looking for me on Mormons2Marry.com—assuming their filters had worked worth kidney beans—we never would have met.

Before I slept, I said a long prayer filled with gratitude. I thanked my Father for the opportunity to meet the artist whose work meant so much to me and for a lovely evening with an interesting man. I thanked Him for being so much wiser than I was when it came to my life, and I told Him that whether or not there was any future for Craig Emory and me, I was grateful to know there were still attractive, accomplished, interesting men who could be attracted to me. I asked Him to bless me to know His will for me.

As I always did when I prayed, I pictured the image from *Embrace;* however, later in the night, when I dreamed, it was Craig Emory's arms I was falling into.

Chapter 15

The rest of the weekend flew by, and I awoke Monday morning tingling with anticipation. I steamed through the morning, a veritable whirlwind of teacherly activity, eagerly awaiting the hour we had scheduled to begin painting our map of the world.

Just before one o'clock, the classroom door opened. When Craig walked through it, I actually felt my heart leap—an expression I've heard before but had always thought overstated. He seemed just as happy to see me.

"Class, this is Mr. Emory," I said, motioning for to him to join me near the chalkboard. "He's going to help us paint our map of the world. Can you welcome him?"

The kids chorused a greeting.

"Then let's get started!" I assigned helpers to carry the paint and brushes, and together Craig and I herded the kids out onto the blacktop, where I turned the project over to him.

He was the epitome of efficient effort as he organized the children and distributed paints and brushes. As I watched him working on our school playground, a light breeze riffling his brown hair while the sun caught the highlights, and his polo shirt stretching tightly across a lean, well-muscled back, I had to stop myself from sighing.

Craig was wonderful with the kids, too. There were times I was sure his fingers itched, wanting to pick up the brushes and do the work himself, but he patiently guided each child through the process of doing his or her very best. He knew the value of having the project belong to the kids and letting them claim ownership. I was impressed with the easy, natural way he motivated the shy children to get involved or encouraged pushier kids to give others a turn. He even had Ellen and Lillian Brenner working calmly together.

When we were finished for the day, Craig helped me clean up while the children went to recess. "Not bad for our first try," he said, looking at our bright green Africa, now nearly complete. "I figure we'll finish this part tomorrow, except for the major bodies of water. I'd suggest we do all the inland water at the same time when we're through with the continents—if that's okay with you."

"Sure. Sounds good," I answered, my mind only half on the project as I watched his large, expressive hands picking up several brushes.

"Shall we move on to Europe next? Asia?"

I shook myself back into the moment. "North America, I think, or the Middle East. We probably should have started with those. Then they could have been really dry before we started painting in the school kids and the soldiers."

He smiled. "No worries there. As long as we don't have rain for a few days, there'll be no trouble with the paints drying. Africa should be plenty dry by tomorrow."

"Good," I replied with a smile. "Thank you so much for coming today, Craig. You were great with the kids. I know you have more important things to do—"

"Nothing more important than this."

"Oh, come on. You have commissions, contracts, beautiful art to create—"

"I'm all caught up on current deadlines and working ahead of schedule on my contracts. Really, Sarah, there's no better place for me to be today. I like kids, and I'm sort of a teacher, too." He picked up a last tube of paint.

"Really?" I should have known that just by watching.

"I coach rugby at the high school near my home."

"No kidding! When do you find time for that?"

"I just volunteer in the afternoons during the season. It's a club sport around here."

"And the season is—?"

"Now. I'll go set up for practice as soon as I leave here. We play one of our major rivals this weekend, and the guys are getting amped up for it."

"No kidding," I repeated, and motioned for Craig to follow me to the classroom so we could wash the brushes. "How did you get into rugby? It isn't exactly a big sport around here."

"No, but it's catching on. I played soccer as a kid, but I always wanted to move up to football—you know, the whole male aggression thing." He grinned, a sort of apology, it seemed, for male aggression. Which was ironic, since he was currently carefully cleaning my students' brushes at the time. "I was okay in football and still played soccer in a spring league, just to stay in shape. Then we got a new coach who brought in rugby, and I was in my element."

He handed me a brush to dry and continued. "It had the aggressiveness of football with the speed and strategy of soccer, and it had one other great benefit—I was good at it. I played through the rest of high school and even played on scholarship in college. Then when I went to Bolivia, I kept in shape with soccer."

"While you were on your mission?"

I must have sounded disapproving, because he replied, "Only when it was allowed, of course. My companions and I often spent part of our P-days kicking around a ball with a bunch of Bolivian or Aymara kids." He finished cleaning the last brush, then carefully wiped the sink clean and leaned against it.

"So now you're the high school rugby coach."

"Assistant coach," he corrected. "Sometimes my work conflicts with an out-of-town game, so I'm happy to let someone else run the show."

"You must enjoy it," I said.

"Love it. It helps me stay fit and gives me a reason to get out of the studio for a little while every day—during spring season, anyway. And I love working with the kids."

"That part is obvious," I assured him.

Long after he left for practice, I was still thinking about the handsome artist who coached rugby and cleaned brushes and sinks. Craig Emory was an enigma, a multi-dimensional puzzle. And I couldn't wait to put more of the pieces together.

* * *

At our family birthday party for Ruth that evening, she pulled me aside to tell me she had received the notice from Mormons2Marry.com and wanted to know how I was taking it. I assured her I would be okay.

"What're you going to do about getting your other four introductions by the end of March?" she asked.

I hedged. "I'm not sure I want them, Ruthie—"

"But you promised me—"

"Ruth, I think I may have met someone."

"You met someone?" she asked, her voice suspicious. "Or you just think *maybe* you met someone."

"Okay, I met someone. I'm just not sure if it means anything yet."

She paused, and a new look crossed her face as she asked, "Really? Honest, Sarah? This isn't just an excuse to dodge your other computer introductions?"

"It's not an excuse."

"So who is he?" Ruth's expression brightened. "What's his name? Is he good and sweet and wonderful and great-looking?"

I beamed. "Yes, yes, yes, and yes, but I'm not ready to talk about him just yet. We just met a couple of days ago."

Ruth narrowed her gaze. "You double-star pinky-swear there really is a guy and that you aren't just ditching out on the dating service?"

"Oh, yeah. There's definitely a guy. I think you'd like him."

"So when do I get to meet him? How soon?"

"Not yet, Ruthie. Give us some time."

She looked so disappointed, and it was her birthday. "Listen. If things don't work out with him right away, I will take Mormons2Marry up on their other four introductions, or at least the next one. Okay? Double-star pinky-swear promise." I made the appropriate gestures from our childhood, crossing my heart twice and locking my little finger with hers.

"Well, okay, as long as you promise," she answered. "And as long as you promise to let me meet him soon, okay?"

"If things are going well, yeah. Soon."

Mom called us in for the birthday cake and candles, and Ruth whispered "soon" again as we rejoined the family.

It was some time later in the evening, as we all sat around the table chatting, that Barbara mentioned something that was "just as funny as Sarah being set up on a computer date with Noah." The rest of the family froze. It was the first anyone had mentioned the incident in front of Ruth, and when Ruthie's jaw dropped, Barbara looked chagrined. "Oops. I'm guessing I wasn't supposed to say that. Ruth hasn't heard yet, I take it?"

Noah and I looked at one another, and Ruth looked from him to me. "Okay," she said, "someone had better start talking. Fast."

So Noah and I told her the whole story, switching off as we went. To Ruthie's credit, she laughed along with the rest of the family when we got to the moment that I walked through the door at Chalet Francaise and found Noah with a yellow rose.

"Okay!" she said. "I finally get it. That's why I couldn't push you into another introduction." She paused. "I should have listened when you warned me about their filters. I'm going to have to get my money back."

* * *

It took a full two weeks of daily one-hour sessions before we had all the continents, mountain ranges, and bodies of water painted, along with the two third-grade children painted in at the side. We traced around Ronny Udall and Emily Ruskin for our models, and Craig made sure they were painted with surprising detail—considering the kids did the work themselves. During the last few days of the project, Mr. Pastori's sixth graders worked on the other side of the world in the mornings, tracing around their teacher and creating a soldier in desert-camouflage fatigues. Throughout all of it, Craig and I worked so well together that it just seemed natural to extend our conversations.

"Are you busy after school?" Craig would usually ask before he left. Then follow up with, "Maybe you could drop by and watch our practice." Or, "How about we grab a pizza and watch the Jazz game?" Or, "There's a Chinese place I've been wanting to check out. Do you like mu shu?"

By the time Mr. Salazar pronounced the project complete and arranged an outdoor assembly in the cold March wind to present it to the school, Craig and I had become accustomed to spending two or three evenings a week and much of each weekend together. I had been to enough rugby practices to know the names of most of his players and had attended enough games to know that rugby could be an exciting spectator sport. I'd learned about props, locks, and flankers, weak side wings and fullbacks, scrums, tries, and conversions—and I had also learned that Craig was an even better kisser than either Justin or Kyle.

We had also discovered that we had a great deal in common. We both loved spicy foods—Thai, Chinese, Mexican—the hotter, the better. We both liked to hike for fun and particularly enjoyed hiking in the mountain canyons, although I hadn't gone hiking at all since I had started teaching. We loved pizza and ice cream and homemade cookies, although we both preferred to eat the dough raw (bad habit, I know). We both looked forward to serving missions, probably more than one, as seniors one day. We both loved to read, although my tastes ran toward nonfiction and the occasional sweet romance, while his tended toward history or techno-thrillers. We both thought the best place on earth was the temple.

I learned that Craig had been buying his art supplies at Allie's Art Mart since it was new, back when Allison was the general manager and only dreaming of buying the store. He was usually in there three or four times a week. When we realized how many times we had crossed paths, it seemed to us less remarkable that we had met and more so that we hadn't met earlier.

We discussed our other commonalities as well, the deeper ones that had helped us feel so close to one another from our first meeting. We talked more of the heartbreaks in our pasts and how much we had struggled with the principle of forgiveness. One evening, as we were splitting a foot-long sub sandwich, I asked him the question that had often crossed my mind. "Craig, I had such a difficult time struggling to forgive the people who hurt me, and your situation was so much worse. How have you managed to let go of it so completely?"

"I'm not sure I've fully let go yet," he said. He set down his food. "I've had a lot of help, though."

"What kind of help?"

"For one thing, I realized that what happened with Lisa was never about me. Lisa was dissatisfied not because I wasn't trying or wasn't earning enough, but because I wasn't Braden. She had wanted him her whole life, and she probably should have married him. I just happened to be in the way when she met him again."

"That's a very powerful insight. It must have been tough to get to that point."

"Oh, it was! Around the same time, I had a good talk with a former bishop who had been a friend of the family for years. I poured out my hurt and anger, and he gave me some very wise counsel."

I began cleaning up. "And that was?"

"He said whenever anyone hurt him, he tried to remember to put himself in that other person's shoes. He said, 'I always ask myself, how would I have to feel to act like that?'"

I thought of the day in the laundry when I'd met Lydia Adams and had suddenly seen Kyle's situation from the other side. "It does make a difference, doesn't it?"

"All the difference in the world. I thought about how I would feel if I were violating my most sacred covenants, if I were hurting the people I loved—how I'd *have* to feel to be saying one thing and living another. It made me feel so sorry for them that I couldn't hurt so much for myself anymore. To some extent, the sympathy replaced the anger."

"You know," I said, "you are a most amazing man."

He smiled that gentle smile I was learning to love. "I'm glad you think so."

We stood and walked toward the door. "Does what happened still jolt you sometimes?"

He didn't answer immediately. He seemed to be choosing his words carefully. "Not so much jolt, at least not anymore. I think the most lasting blow was to my confidence."

"Your confidence? But you said you realized it wasn't about you."

"It wasn't, mostly, but parts of it were." He paused, looked away. "You see, I prayed about whether I should marry Lisa, and I felt my answer had been confirmed. When it turned out so badly . . . well, I sometimes second-guess my decisions now."

"Ah, I understand. I felt the same way. In my case, I was probably just hearing the answer I wanted."

"I don't feel that way. I feel I was really inspired to marry her."

I took a moment to think about that. "Perhaps you were. Maybe, since the other man was already married, you were giving her the nobler option. If she had kept her covenants, you two might have been happy."

"Maybe," he said, but he didn't seem convinced.

* * *

It was a few days later that I invited Craig to visit my home, an impromptu "why don't you join us?" sort of thing that had him sitting down for cricket soup and corn bread with Shari, Kerry, and me while Harry wound around his feet. He complimented my little house and the colors I'd chosen, happily bounced Kerry on his knee as if he did it every day, and slipped a bit of hamburger to Harry, though the cat didn't have a clue what to do with it. He seemed like one of the family when he chimed in to help with cleanup.

Still, I had not yet introduced him to my family, and Ruth was beginning to nag about the pinky-swear promise I'd made. I hadn't yet been to Craig's home either. We always met at my school or at his or in other public places. I was beginning to wonder if the starving artist was afraid to show me his humble digs, so I decided to broach the subject myself.

About a week later, Craig was having his second or third dinner at my place. Shari was out with Noah, so it was just the two of us, and I was serving up my first attempt at Shari's caramel fudge cake when I said, "You know, you haven't cooked for me yet." I cocked a brow. "You do cook, don't you?"

He grinned, recognizing the bait but biting anyway. "Nothing to brag about, certainly nothing like this cake, but I can keep body and soul together." There was a meaningful pause. "How about Friday night?"

"Sounds good," I answered. "What can I bring?"

"Just yourself. It will be my treat."

I swallowed my last bite. "You know, I've been curious about your house, about the sort of place a working artist chooses to live."

"It's a little different," he said.

"Different how?"

He just grinned. "You'll see."

Craig's home was in fact unlike any I'd ever seen. Way back in the Brigham Young days, a group of farmers had come to this end of the valley, now known as Riverton, to raise sugar beets and hay. They had organized a small ward and built a chapel of good red brick. Over the years the town had grown up around it, but by the 1970s, the little chapel no longer met the needs of a modern-sized ward. The church built a new building and sold the old brick one with the stained-glass windows to a Protestant congregation.

By the turn of the century, the Protestant congregation was in financial distress and the building was in disrepair. The little church was on and off the market for a few years and even got to the "sale pending" stage a couple of times, but the deals always fell through. Then, just before Craig's divorce was final, he used his new art income to purchase, gut, and renovate the old brick church.

The small chapel, stained glass still in place, had become his studio. Drop cloths and easels holding large canvases were strategically placed where the light was best. Cabinets full of paints and materials stood along the walls beneath the arching windows, and the area that had once contained the organ, podium, and choir loft now held a half dozen finished paintings, awaiting delivery to a client or presentation at Craig's next show.

The cultural hall, which Craig assured me had "never been big enough for full-court basketball," had been organized into a family room with a free-standing fireplace, a dining area, and an office work space. One end opened into the refurbished kitchen. Classrooms off one side of the building had become bedrooms with baths between them, and the few rooms on the other side had been converted into a formal entry, a formal living room—where *Embrace* was prominently displayed—a guest room and bath, and a triple-car garage that opened off the side street.

In the parking area, Craig had torn up the blacktop and had brought in truckloads of topsoil and composted steer manure. He now had the beginnings of a small family orchard and truck garden, carefully fenced in and set up on automatic watering systems. He'd included a broad stretch of lawn as well. It was all lovely, roomy, and creative—not the starving artist digs at all, but a spacious home and workplace for a successful artist. I also noticed, though I chose not to mention it right away, that both the house and yard were ideal for a large family.

"It's beautiful," I told him, my admiration obvious. "Creative and artistic, but homey, too. You've done some amazing work here."

"I'm glad you like it," he said. His pleasure in my admiration was equally obvious, and I realized my approval had been important to him. He guided me toward the kitchen. "Dinner awaits you, madam. With a bit of luck, it's edible."

It turned out Craig was more than a passable cook. His linguine with meatballs and marinara sauce rivaled the best I'd eaten anywhere, and he had also tossed a delicious green salad. He added some garlic bread and finished the meal off with strawberries and cream. It was simple but impressive. When we had finished eating, Craig built a fire and we cuddled on the leather sofa, his arm around me and my head on his shoulder, just talking. It seemed we'd never run out of things to say to each other.

He shared his pride in his parents, who were currently serving a full-time mission in Belgium, and his older brother, Ryan, who had just become president of an East Coast company that specialized in medical supplies and equipment. I shared stories from my brothers' missions and from my parents' plans to serve when Dad retired in another few years.

He told me of his sorrow for his younger brother, Phil, who had stopped attending church the day he turned eighteen and had recently moved in with his third live-in girlfriend. Then he added, "You know, I've felt a lot of guilt about Phil."

"You have? Why?"

"He was at a critical crossroads around the time of my divorce. He'd just had a painful split from the girl he thought he'd marry, and he was even talking about coming back to church. Then my divorce happened . . . I've often worried that might have served a part in turning him away."

"You know you can't take responsibility for his choices. You couldn't help what happened."

"No, but I do feel sorry for it."

I let that sink in for a moment as I watched the fire. "I think I have an inkling how you may feel," I said, then I told him about my cousin Maddie, a lovely girl whom no one in our family had been in contact with since she stormed away six years before. We empathized with one another over the sorrow in our families, and then shared a few funny family stories to lighten the mood.

Finally I felt bold enough to ask, "Craig, I can't help noticing that there are at least five bedrooms here—"

"Six," he answered, "including the master bedroom and the guest room on the other side."

"And there's a nice, fenced-in yard where children could play . . ."

He didn't respond.

"I know you were just finalizing your divorce when you bought the place, and yet you renovated it to house a large family."

It seemed a long while before Craig answered. "Let's just say I was going on faith. You know, 'faith precedes the miracle.'"

I dropped my voice. "Were you hoping to win Lisa back?"

"Oh, no. That was clearly, irrevocably over." He paused. "No. I was looking toward the future."

"The future, huh?" I cuddled closer, feeling warm and hopeful.

There was another charged pause until he said, "So tell me, what made you decide to be a teacher?" And we talked again of our work.

To my astonishment, I learned that Craig had never thought of himself as a celebrity—even the minor kind. He was always surprised when someone recognized his name or asked for his autograph. Sometime during that Friday evening, as we sat talking in front of his fireplace, I left behind my hero worship for the perceptive and talented artist called Craig Emory and began falling in love with the man.

* * *

April brought a spate of rainstorms—though not quite enough to break the drought—an important rugby win, and more time with Craig. Time and increasing familiarity gave us the opportunity to discover some of our differences. For starters, there was the red versus blue rivalry. Although he had completed his master's degree at the Y, his undergraduate work had all been done at the University of Utah, where he had his rugby scholarship and where his father had taught for years in the physics department. Craig frankly declared the U had better sports teams. I was a BYU grad and fan, Cougar blue clear through, so we had to agree to disagree about college sports.

Then there were our human quirks. I learned that Craig could get highly focused when inspired by a project—so focused he forgot appointments or dates, and sometimes even forgot to eat or get a glass of water for hours at a stretch.

He learned I often got grumpy when I hadn't slept enough. He also learned I got moody and downright unpleasant when I'd been dieting to lose nine pounds before Noah and Shari's wedding and Shari served homemade ice cream. I learned he could get edgy and snappish when a painting wasn't going well. We both learned we enjoyed one another's company even when focused, grumpy, moody, or snappish. We admitted we were falling in love.

By general conference we were beginning to talk marriage, though only in vague, abstract, "maybe-someday" terms. Craig was especially cautious about committing, since he had tried that once and it hadn't turned out well, but still, we were beginning to think about spending our eternities together. It seemed like time and past time for Craig to meet my family.

So far the only Kimball who had even seen him was Noah, who had become a permanent fixture at my house. The timing had just never been right for him to meet the whole family. I thought maybe we'd manage an introduction during conference, but Craig had committed weeks earlier to fly to his brother's place in Maryland over conference weekend, so we missed that opportunity, too.

Conference was wonderful. I loved the messages taught by humble, loving servants of God. I also loved the family time, although I found myself wishing I had someone to defend me from Baby Ruth. Mormons2Marry.com had now closed its virtual doors, and Ruth had given up on getting her money back, but she kept reminding me of my pinky-swear promise.

In truth, I had begun to wonder if Craig was avoiding meeting my family. That next Friday, when he and I doubled with Noah and Shari for dinner and a movie, I enlisted my brother's help. We both invited Craig to join us when we celebrated Josh's birthday the next week. He said he wished very much he could be there but couldn't make it; he had a show in Cedar City. Just when I was about to ask him whether he *wanted* to meet my relatives, Noah invited him for the next week to celebrate Deb's big thirty-five, and he readily accepted.

That's when I started getting nervous. Would he like my family? How could he not? Would they like him? What was there not to like? At the same time, I couldn't forget my own past prejudice. Maybe other members of my family felt the same way. Or had Shari broken that barrier? Would my brothers find it difficult to accept a man who made his living by painting? But I could point out that he coached rugby, too . . . I worried and fussed, wondering how Deb's birthday would go.

To pacify Ruth, I told her I was bringing "a friend," and she quickly alerted the whole family about "Sarah's new guy." They were all watching at the windows when we walked up from the car, hand in hand. The expression on Ruth's face told me exactly what she thought of Craig. Who could blame her? He was a handsome man.

I presented Craig Emory to the Kimball crowd and the Kimballs, one by one, to Craig. He charmed them all, as I knew he would, remembered many of their names through the evening, helped in the kitchen, played with the little ones, talked sports with my dad and brothers, and even managed to rock Lauren to sleep when she threw a tired tantrum at the dinner table. The icing on the cake was the gift he presented to our birthday girl. When we all had sung to Deb and she had served chocolate cake to everyone, various family members brought out their gifts—the kind of small tokens we Kimballs were accustomed to sharing.

Then Craig said, "If you'll all stay put for just a minute, I have my gift in the truck," and stepped out the front door. Family members all looked at me, but I raised my shoulders in a who-knows gesture. Craig soon returned bearing a large, flat box.

As Deb opened it, she gasped, and her eyes filled with tears. Then she showed Brian, who gulped and teared up, too. His voice was husky as he said, "Thank you. I don't know how you did this, but thank you so much." Then Deb turned the box to show the whole family a gift I hadn't seen and hadn't even realized was in the back of the pickup's cab.

It was a large portrait of Deb and Brian, painted with the photographic detail that was such a hallmark of Craig's work but without the few wrinkles on Deb's forehead or the gray at Brian's temples. They were smiling and looked so happy together. It was beautifully matted and framed, ready for hanging, an absolute treasure. As Deb showed us the painting, there were gasps and appreciative murmurs from the whole family, and then I asked, though my voice was thick, too, "Craig, how did you do this?"

"Remember a couple of weeks ago when Noah invited me here tonight? You showed me your family portrait that same evening. You were telling me how you wanted me to meet them."

I only vaguely remembered that moment, but I nodded.

"I had you point out Deb and her husband. When you were in the kitchen, I sketched them from the photo and made a few notes. Then, well—" He gestured toward the canvas. If I had been impressed before, I was now speechless.

So were all the Kimballs, except Noah, who quickly asked if Craig was coming to *his* birthday party in May. Everyone laughed. Throughout the next hour as we closed down the party and helped to tidy up, people kept walking by the portrait—touching its frame, talking about it, marveling. Everyone spoke to Craig at various moments, admiring his talent and thanking him for his work. This meeting had been a long time in coming, but it was definitely worth it. Clearly Craig had won my family's hearts. He already had mine.

Chapter 16

The following week, Shari graduated—a credentialed teacher at last—and I took a personal day to attend her convocation. Craig skipped one of his team's last league games to come with me, and we drove down to Provo together. Noah was there, of course, holding Kerry while her mommy walked across the stage. Shari's younger sister came out from California, and I finally got to meet Shari's parents, who had kindly arranged a luncheon for all of us after the convocation. After watching Shari's mother in action, I understood where Shari got her sensible, feet-on-the-ground approach to life. I liked Sister Wallace immediately. Brother Wallace was adorable, too, although Shari seemed a bit annoyed that he remembered so many embarrassing stories from her childhood, all of which he wanted to share with Noah.

At the post-ceremony luncheon, there were cards and gifts, an occasional check, and lots of fun and friends and laughter. There was even a card from Shari's ex-in-laws, the Crawfords, the people she referred to as Kerry's other grandparents, who offered their congratulations and best wishes for a great career.

"So now that you've found Mr. Perfect, what are you going to do about your career?" asked Shari's friend Trina, who was graduating in the same class. "Are you still planning to teach?"

Shari and Noah exchanged a meaningful look before Shari answered, "We're still deciding that. Maybe, after the wedding—"

"And when is that, exactly?" Trina cut in.

Shari's smile faded. "I only wish I knew."

Sister Wallace reminded me of my own mother when she tactfully changed the subject, but we had all noticed that the time when Noah and Shari planned to be married was almost upon us, and there still was no date for their wedding. The cancellation of her prior sealing had not yet come through.

Shari and Noah were talking about their situation that evening when I got home. Craig and I had visited the new exhibit in BYU's Museum of Art, where he had been thoroughly in his element discussing the lasting influence of the French impressionists on the art world. Then we had wandered around campus for awhile, sharing our past Y experiences, before he took me to dinner at his favorite seafood place in Provo. He had an early appointment the next day and some paperwork he needed to complete before he went, so we said good-night at the door and I let myself in, just in time to hear Noah say, "What do you think is taking so long?"

I peeked around the corner. Shari was sitting at the dining table, and Noah was pacing around her.

"I don't know!" Shari replied, frustration coloring her voice. "The paperwork was complete within days—even Ken's letter. The bishop warned me that it could take as long as three months, but he thought it would be closer to two—"

"It's been more than two already."

"I know, Noah."

"We can't even make plans—"

"I *know*, Noah."

He sighed, and there was a long pause as he composed himself. He sounded calmer when he said, "I'm sorry, babe. I know you're as anxious about this as I am. I just want us to be married, that's all."

Shari stood to meet him. "You know I want that, too."

"It's time," Noah said, and they moved into one another's arms.

I stuck my head into the kitchen. "Roommate and sister announcing her presence!" I declared, and they reluctantly separated.

"Hi, Sarah," Shari said at the same moment Noah said, "I didn't hear you, sis."

"That's why I announced myself," I said, and sat down at the table. "I take it there's still no word yet . . ."

"Not yet," Shari answered tightly.

An awkward silence followed. Both Noah and Shari remained standing. It took me a moment to get the clue.

"Well, I'm tired," I said, then stood up and stretched, yawning broadly to make it look good. "It's been quite a day, hasn't it? Congratulations, Shari." I gave her a quick hug and made my exit, retreating to my bedroom to record the day in my journal. I didn't know how late they stayed up, but I could still hear the low, unhappy murmur of their voices when I drifted off to sleep.

* * *

As April turned into May, we still hadn't heard any word of Shari's sealing cancellation, and emotions were close to the surface. The approaching end of the school year gave me plenty to do at work, so I frequently used that as an excuse to stay late, avoiding both Noah and Shari. I watched Craig's team lose a heartbreaking season-ender in the league semifinals and went with him to the team's final awards dinner, watching with pride as he spoke apprecia-tively of each of the boys on his team. He knew them all so well, and they all clearly adored him.

Noah's birthday was on May third, and Craig came with me to the family dinner and even came through on the gift Noah had joked about—a stunning portrait of Noah and Shari that flattered them both and seemed to capture how very in love they were, despite their frustrations about the wedding. He explained it was painted from a digital shot he had snapped when we were all together one evening. Neither Noah nor Shari could remember posing for a photo, and neither had expected the portrait, despite Noah's teasing. They were as overwhelmed and grateful as Deb and Brian had been.

"Are you going to do this for all the couples in the family?" Josh prompted. "Our anniversary is coming up next week."

Craig grinned. "I can probably get to all of you in time."

My mom gave me a quick look, eyebrows raised, and I shrugged in response. By now the family had come to see us as a couple and seemed to expect Craig at family events, but Craig had made no clear statement of his plans, and I didn't want to presume. I had thought of praying about whether or not I should marry Craig, but it seemed premature, since he hadn't asked me. It helped to know that my family was crazy about him.

The following day was Monday, and it was my turn to plan family home evening, although I had handed off the biggest part by asking Noah to give the lesson. He arrived early and joined me in the kitchen, where I had started dinner. He was eager for Shari to join us, but a bit timid, too. "We had quite a row last night. How was she doing when you last saw her?" he asked on his third or fourth pacing tour.

"I haven't seen her yet today—was this about the wedding?"

He sighed and started his next tour of the kitchen. "I just don't understand the holdup. We should have been married by now."

"I know—Wait, Noah, she's here."

As we listed to Shari's car pulling in, I think we both braced ourselves. We didn't need to. Shari burst through the door grinning, Kerry on one hip. "Great news!"

Noah brightened. "The cancellation came through?"

"Finally!"

Noah dashed across the room, grabbed both Shari and Kerry, and swung them in a wide circle. Then he lowered Kerry to the floor, said, "Excuse us for a minute, honey," and kissed Shari tenderly and thoroughly. My face warmed and I grabbed Kerry's hand. "Come on, punkin. Let's go see if we can find Harry." I led her out of the room.

"They kiss a lot," Kerry observed. "Look, there's Harry right there!"

When we came back, Noah and Shari were chatting companionably at the dining table. Shari's relief was matched only by Noah's. They had set their date for June fifteenth.

"I still say it should be sooner," Noah said as Kerry and I sat down.

Shari shook her head. "That's barely time to get out the invitations."

"Then let's just call everybody!"

Shari smiled. "June fifteenth is a great day to be married."

"*Any* day is a great day to be married," Noah said, and kissed her emphatically.

After a moment, I hustled them from the table and began to clear things away so we could set places for dinner. It wasn't until I picked up the day's mail that I remembered. "Oh, you got mail, Shari—

including one big envelope that looks like it could be important." I handed it to her.

She looked at the return address and her eyes widened. "Oh, my. Oh, my! Wish me luck, everyone," she said and then she carefully opened it. A few seconds later, she squealed and threw her hands into the air. "He signed! Oh, Noah! Ken signed the papers!"

"Really?" Noah ran to read over Shari's shoulder. "Oh, honey, this is wonderful!" Then they were kissing again.

I cleared my throat. "Uh, does somebody want to tell me—"

Noah broke the kiss long enough to say, "Shari's ex signed the paperwork. He's going to let me adopt Kerry."

"That's wonderful!" I said, grabbing Kerry up into my arms. "Noah's going to be your daddy, sweetheart!"

Kerry alone appeared unmoved. She simply smiled and said, "Mommy already told me."

"As soon as it's final, we can have you sealed to us, baby." Shari took Kerry from my arms into hers, and then she pulled me in, too. We shared another group hug and a shower of kisses that tasted of happy tears.

* * *

I saw Craig twice during that next week, on Tuesday evening when I went with him to visit an older, widowed sister he home taught, and again on Friday when he picked me up at the end of the school day for dinner and a movie. We also spent most of Saturday together, hiking up to the reservoir in Bells Canyon. It was the first time I'd been hiking in months, so Craig promised to take it easy on me, but his idea of "easy" was a bit different from mine. The hike was less than four miles, but all uphill—more than four thousand vertical feet. By three o'clock, my legs were noodles and my lungs felt as if someone had been sandpapering them from the inside.

"I'm done," I groaned as we reached the water.

"Ah, too bad. I was thinking about going dancing tonight."

"Don't let me slow you down." I sank onto the cement piling near the dam. "You have a fine time."

He chuckled. "How about dinner instead? My place."

"Can't make that, either."

He lifted one eyebrow. "You have a hot date?"

"Sort of. Mom planned a little get-together—Shari, me, Deb, Ruth, any of the sisters-in-law who can make it. We're going to brainstorm ideas to help Shari with her wedding planning."

"Don't most brides do that themselves?"

"I suppose so, but Shari hasn't had a lot of time to plan, what with earning all A's in her grad work and doing student teaching. And besides, she and Noah are working with a fairly tight budget." I stopped for breath in the thin mountain air. "It would help if she could make up her mind about colors."

He looked thoughtful. "Maybe I can help."

I smiled. "Don't tell me you're a wedding planner, too."

"No, but I work with color every day."

"That's true. You do," I answered, beginning to see potential.

And that was how Craig ended up the only man around my mom's dining table that evening. He approached the planning of wedding colors with the same intensity and careful preparation he gave to everything else.

"I can't believe he brought paint chips," Wendy said as Craig unloaded a whole box of color samples.

"Where did you *find* this guy?" Denise asked in mock astonishment.

Ruth said, "I don't care where you found him. Just go back and find another one for me, okay?" Her remark made Craig smile and got us started laughing as we began working on color choices.

"The problem," Shari explained, "is trying to match mismatched colors. My sister, with her fabulous blond hair, looks stunning in tangerine orange, so that's what she wants to wear."

"That is a problem," said Barbara. "There aren't many people who look great in orange." We all nodded agreement.

Shari went on. "Noah just loves the color—"

"Purple." Mom, Deb, Ruth, and I all answered for her. Noah had been notorious in the family ever since he had painted his whole bedroom in deep purple when he was fourteen. Mom had needed three coats of primer before she could repaint it while he was on his mission.

"Yes, purple," Shari confirmed with a grin. "So you see—"

"You're the bride," Mom said. "What colors do *you* like?"

Shari sighed. "I just like color. Anything bright and cheerful is fine with me. If we went with the tangerine, I could see using yellow and coral to complement it. If we chose purple, we could have different shades of lavender, violet, orchid, deep blue . . . I want everyone to be happy with the choices, but orange and purple? Huh-uh."

"Gotta agree with you there," said Denise.

We were all murmuring our agreement when Craig said, "I don't know about that. Have you ever seen a bird of paradise?"

We turned to look at him. "Huh?" Shari asked. "Those weird birds?"

"The *flower* called the 'bird of paradise.'"

"Well, yeah, I guess . . ." Denise answered.

"It's blazing tangerine orange with a deep purple center."

My mother answered, "Yes, I've seen those flowers. Aunt Carol has some in her yard in Phoenix. They're beautiful."

"They *are* beautiful," Craig agreed. "And the artist who put those colors together knew exactly what He was doing."

"He certainly did." Denise spoke for all of us.

Shari still looked doubtful. "I don't think we can afford anything that unusual. Isn't that a very expensive flower?"

"I can solve that," he said. "Let me buy the flowers. It will be my wedding gift."

Shari gasped. "Oh no, Craig, we can't ask you to take on that expen—"

"You're not asking. I volunteered."

"Really, Craig. I don't think—"

"I'm going to do it," Craig said. "It's settled."

Shari seemed ready to argue, but Mom laid a hand on her arm. "Really, dear, just look at him. He wants to help."

"I don't know if I can arrange flowers like that," said Wendy, who had done all the flowers for her own wedding and several others since.

"I can help," Craig offered. "It will be part of the gift."

Denise stared. "Don't tell me you do flower arranging, too?"

He chuckled. "Only a little. Call it a survival skill. A student artist paints a lot of still lifes before he's allowed to move on."

"Where did you *find* this guy?" Barbara asked again.

I grinned. "Allie's Art Mart."

"Have you used birds of paradise before?" Wendy asked as Craig started arranging his paint chips on the table. "I wouldn't even know what kinds of flowers to combine with them, or how to arrange other items around them."

"I haven't worked with them before, but I'm getting an idea," Craig said. "Exotic flowers could work well with a kind of minimalist, Asian theme. Here, look." He grabbed a pad and started sketching while the women in my family all exchanged astonished looks over his head. When we left Mom's later that evening, Shari had an exotic, elegant reception all planned on paper, and I had gained an even greater appreciation for the man beside me.

"You're sure making a great impression on my family," I said as he drove me home.

He grinned. "That's great, but I'm really hoping to impress you."

"Oh, you've done that. Honestly, is there anything you *can't* do?"

"Balance a checkbook," he said, guiltily.

"No kidding!" I had a fleeting thought of his beautiful home and wondered about the size of his mortgage.

"It's embarrassing, but the same accountant I hire for my company also keeps my personal records. If she didn't, I'd be in a world of trouble."

"Craig, I'm stunned!" I teased him. "Except for that unreasonable obsession with U of U sports, I thought you were practically perfect."

"I can't waltz, either."

I covered my ears in mock horror. "Oh, no. Say it isn't so!"

"Now that you know the bitter truth, will you still want to be seen with me?" He looked so wonderful with that teasing grin, I'd have leaned over and kissed him if we hadn't just turned onto 90th South, where the traffic was predictably heavy.

"I don't know." I tried to look somber. "Such behavior could bring utter disgrace, but I have never let social stricture tarnish my decisions."

"Then you'll go with me to Uintah County over the Memorial Day weekend?"

At first I thought I must have misheard him, but I replayed the words in my head and they still came out the same way. I could feel my brow furrowing. "Craig, did you just ask me to go away with you for the weekend?"

"Well, yeah, I guess—just not the way it sounded."

"Maybe you'd better back up and explain what you have in mind."

So he told me about the contract he had won to do a major painting in the new county building in Vernal, the Uintah County seat. He was just now completing the work—a sort of montage of the county's pioneer history along with chamber of commerce–type scenes of tourist sites, dinosaurs, crops, and so forth that made that corner of Utah worth visiting. "I'm supposed to deliver the painting on the Friday before Memorial Day," he said. "Then there will be an unveiling ceremony on Saturday, and they want me to be there."

I nodded and he continued. "I thought it would be fun if you could come with me. We could go to the community picnic, maybe visit Dinosaur National Park or Flaming Gorge, attend church there on Sunday, do some hiking in the Uintas . . . And there would be a lot of driving time for just talking, too."

"Is there something in particular you want to talk about?"

"Could be," he said with an air of mystery. "Of course you'd need to take a personal day off from teaching for that Friday, but you'll already have time off for the rest of the weekend."

Addressing my primary concern, he added, "I've booked a room at a little bed-and-breakfast there, but if you can come, I'll book two rooms instead."

"Of course," I answered sensibly, but my mind was racing. Even with separate rooms, a weekend away seemed a bit risky—at least, compared to my usual conservative behavior. There was the whole "appearance of evil" argument, after all. And aside from that, Memorial Day was only days away from the end of the school year and a terrible time to ask for a personal day. But what did Craig have in mind when he said there were things for us to talk about?

"That's two weeks away, right?" I asked, stalling for time.

"Right. Two weeks from yesterday is my delivery deadline. We could leave after work the day before."

"That's Thursday, the, uh . . ." I was trying to count on my fingers.

"Thursday the twenty-first. We'd be back by Monday evening."

Maybe it wouldn't have seemed monumental to anyone else, but I couldn't help feeling there was a lot riding on my choice. I wanted more time to think about it. "Let me check with Mr. Salazar about the personal time," I said. "I'll see him sometime on Monday—if that's soon enough."

"Sure," he said. "I don't think all the rooms in Vernal will sell out before then."

Then something clicked. "Wait. I don't think I'd need a room. My mom's Aunt Miriam lives in Vernal. I'm sure she'd let me stay with her." The idea of a chaperone made the whole escapade seem a little less daring.

"That sounds great," Craig said. I was beginning to think so, too.

Chapter 17

Monday morning found me eager to talk with Mr. Salazar. I caught him in the office during lunch and told him I'd like to take a personal day on the Friday before Memorial Day weekend. By then my only fear was that my principal might object, but he just glanced at my file to be sure I had the personal day coming (I did), and immediately gave his okay. He even said that he knew of substitutes who'd be glad for a day's work and that he hoped I had a great weekend.

By the time Craig joined my little household for family home evening, I had already cleared my stay with my Great-Auntie Miriam, who said she'd be thrilled to have me with her even if I already had plans to be busy and away during most of my visit. Craig seemed delighted with the news. Shari and Noah teased us about going away for the weekend, but only a little, and neither of them seemed the least bit scandalized. That cleared any lingering doubts I had, and we eagerly began planning our trip.

The ensuing two weeks were so full that Craig and I didn't see each other as often as we'd have liked. I had more long days at school, as well as some evenings with end-of-school parent programs and final report cards to compute. (With the help of Ellen's tutoring, Lillian Brenner was actually getting a B in spelling!) Shari kept me busy as well, taking me with her to visit cake-makers and dress alterers and party rental shops. Meanwhile, Craig was balancing making the final touches on his huge painting for Uintah County—he called it *Discovery*—with the start of a new project for a natural history museum in one of the southern states. It was to depict the Four Corners plateau as it might have looked during the days of the wooly mammoth and saber-tooth tiger. In moments of creative downtime as Craig completed *Discovery,* he was researching what naturalists had postulated about that earlier time and place.

We still managed to catch quick moments together, but most of our contact during those two weeks was through telephone calls, e-mail, and text messaging. All the while, Craig kept dropping tantalizing hints. When I texted him about going with Shari to pick her cake, he suggested I should think about the wedding cake I wanted—someday. When I told him she looked splendid in her temple-ready gown, he said he had imagined how lovely I would look as a bride—someday. When I told him we had arranged the rental of the few items we still needed to complete his minimalist Asian design, he said I should be thinking about how I would want my reception to look—and he didn't even add the "someday." My prayers became more focused as I prepared for the long drive to Vernal and back and the conversation I hoped we would have.

I wanted to know. This time I really wanted to *know.* I had asked before, when Kyle proposed, and I thought I had received my answer. I had been confused and frustrated when the breakup came. It had taken me some time to realize that I had been listening only for what I wanted. This time I wanted to be certain I was making the right choice for both Craig and me—the choice our Heavenly Father would have us make.

The Sunday night before the trip, as I prayed about Craig and whether we were right for each other, I had a vivid memory of the moment when I had told my mother about my broken engagement and my broken heart. As I sobbed on her shoulder, she had said, "Honey, maybe the Lord just doesn't want you to marry Kyle." At the time it had made me furious. I had answered in a way that seemed prideful and haughty now, telling her I felt certain the Lord had not arranged for Kyle to get his girlfriend pregnant.

Now that I had come to know my Savior better, I realized He had known that Kyle and I weren't right for each other and had used what we had given Him to lead us both in separate directions. Of course I was right about the basics—the Lord didn't arrange for anyone to commit sins. Surely He would have preferred for Kyle and me to separate because we were listening to the Spirit, not because Beth was expecting. Yet I understood now that in His infinite love and compassion, He was able to use even sins and mistakes to bless me as I tried, however feebly, to seek His will.

This conviction was confirmed for me that night, when I got an e-mail from an old BYU study buddy. It was one of those general announcements sent out to everyone in his address book to say he had a new e-mail address, and I guess I was still in his address book. Sam and I had been in a geology course together just about the time I had started seeing Kyle, and since he had come from Kyle's St. Louis stake, he had known us both.

I sent back a quick note just to say hi, and we exchanged a few messages. That was how I learned that Kyle and Beth had a "real cute" little boy and that they planned to be sealed in the St. Louis Temple sometime before the end of the year. I wrote back, telling Sam I was delighted for the Lewises, and happily realized I meant it. It sounded like Kyle and Beth were good for one another, even if they hadn't discovered it in the best of ways. Then I realized with a little jolt that if Kyle hadn't left me for her, I likely never would have met Craig Emory. I pondered these thoughts as I prepared for our trip to Vernal and prayed for my answer.

Craig was supposed to join us for FHE the next night but bowed out at the last moment. The huge rack he used to carry paintings in the back of his truck had developed some kind of problem which he tried to explain, but I didn't understand. When Craig called me, he was busy with a soldering iron, making the structure more reliable to carry his treasured art, and he didn't want to leave the project until he was certain we could safely take *Discovery* with us when we left for Vernal. Because of a Relief Society board meeting the next evening, we didn't see other each on Tuesday, either. By the time he picked me up just after I got home on Wednesday, we were eager to see each other and spent some time just basking in one another's company.

Our task for the evening was simple: We were going grocery shopping. We'd pick up some snacks for the trip, make sure we had plenty of drinking water, and buy some good batteries for our flashlights—just in case. After we were finished shopping, we'd spend a few minutes going over our schedule and plans for the weekend. It all seemed fairly cut-and-dry, and yet I found myself enjoying it more than any date we'd been on in a long while. It was so good just to be with Craig, to spend time with him. To my astonishment, I realized that even more than Shari, even more than Jeanie, even more than my sisters or my mom, Craig Emory had become my best friend. It was a blessing just to be with him.

This realization struck me as profoundly moving. It wasn't quite the witness of the Spirit that I had been seeking, but it was a kind of answer all its own. The peaceful, quiet happiness that I felt just being with Craig was unlike anything I had ever known before. It seemed only normal that I hadn't felt like this with Justin, whom I had not known either long enough or well enough to love like this, but I hadn't had these feelings with Kyle, either. This was a degree and depth of love unlike anything I had even thought possible. My heart swelling with emotion, my eyes beginning to tear, I took Craig's arm as we entered the grocery store near his home in Riverton, and he put his hand over mine.

We walked like that, up and down the rows, choosing some snacks we both liked and talking about our trip. Each time one of us broke contact to look at something or reach for something or lift something down off a shelf, we came back into the same position. It felt like a dance with steps we both knew so well that we didn't have to think about them as we walked together, talking quietly, me holding Craig's arm and the two of us looking at one another as if the world had been created for us alone. It was then that a tall, slim, stately woman in a fashionable skirt and high heels walked around the corner into our aisle and I felt Craig's arm go rigid.

I had never seen Lisa, nor had I seen pictures of her, but I knew who she was the moment I looked at her. And even if my inward signaling system had not been working up to par, I'd have known from Craig's reaction—the sudden stiffness, the way he stopped walking and froze where he stood, the fact that the color drained from his face and the veins in his neck stood out as though they were ready to burst. My own throat tightened as the woman looked up and saw us, then stopped a few feet away, looking almost as shell-shocked as Craig did. Her quiet "Hello, Craig," seemed anticlimactic.

"Hello," he managed. He put his arm around me and drew me closer. I wasn't sure whether the gesture was possessive or protective.

Then he said, "I'd like you to meet Sarah Kimball. Sarah, this is my . . . this is Lisa, Lisa, uh—"

"Mannion." She supplied the name to fill in the blank.

"Lisa Mannion," Craig repeated, unnecessarily adding, "my ex-wife."

We all stood there, awkwardly looking at one another, until I couldn't stand it any longer. I stepped around the shopping cart and offered my hand. "Hello, Lisa," I said.

She answered, "Hello, uh, Samantha, is it?"

"It's Sarah. Sarah Kimball," I said evenly. I couldn't decide whether I wanted to snub her and simply walk away or pull her hair and start a catfight in the crackers-and-cookies aisle. Instead I stepped back behind the grocery cart next to Craig, who pulled me in tightly against him.

"You look good," Lisa said, her eyes on Craig alone.

He looks wonderful! I wanted to shout, followed by something like, *You hurt him enough. Leave him alone!* I held my tongue, of course. After a few meaningless pleasantries, she said, "Good to meet you, Samantha," and I managed a mumbled, "You too," as she walked past us.

She disappeared around the corner and we stood there, as still as the boxes on the shelves. After a long moment, Craig said, "Let's check out," and started for the cash registers.

That's when the whole evening shifted into fast forward. I knew Craig had been shaken by the encounter, but it seemed as if he couldn't get rid of me fast enough. He hurried through checkout, rushed through an abbreviated discussion of the weekend's schedule in the cab of his truck (we had been planning to go back to his house), then hustled me home with some excuse about how we both needed sleep. Even his goodnight kiss was perfunctory, seemingly offered more out of obligation than affection. Stepping through my front door was like stepping back through the looking glass, back from an alternate universe into my former reality. I stood staring out the window, watching as Craig drove away, uncertain whether to feel more devastated or furious. Wasn't it enough that Lisa had ruined so much already? Did she have to ruin this, too? Did she have to ruin *us?*

Even as I had these thoughts, I knew they were unfair. Lisa had stopped at the grocery store to pick up a few things just as we had. It was no more her intention to ruin our evening than it was ours to ruin hers. Yet ruin it she had. I wondered how she felt about the encounter and whether it could possibly be bothering her as much as it was me.

* * *

Somehow I finally slept, and somehow I got through school the next day. By the time Craig came to pick me up that next afternoon, I had almost persuaded myself that nothing was different, that everything between us would be just fine—almost. As we drove away together, it seemed clear that Craig too was trying to regain the homey, comfortable ease we'd always had. The problem was, he was trying too hard. Somehow everything one of us said turned into something prickly or difficult, every subject became sore, and every idea seemed to rub the other person the wrong way. After awhile I just sat looking out the window, feeling as desolate as the desert landscape, trying not to say anything at all.

That was when Craig said, "Look, Sarah, we need to talk about something."

I felt a stab of grief. For the past couple of weeks, I'd been looking forward to this conversation, and yet, now that it had begun, I knew it wasn't going to go as I had hoped.

"Yes," I answered, trying for an encouraging smile. "We have a lot to talk about."

Even though I knew that the energy between us today had all been uncomfortably negative, and even though I now felt certain that Craig wasn't ready to propose, I certainly wasn't expecting what came next. He looked away, keeping his eyes on the road as he said, "I've been thinking maybe we're hurrying all of this way too fast. Maybe we need to slow it down for awhile, maybe even see other people . . ."

See other people? Wasn't that code for "I want to break up?" Inside my own head I could hear myself screaming, "No, not again! This can't be happening!" I felt tears sting my eyes as my throat tensed in a knot of grief. Ironically, it was then, at the precise moment my dating relationship with Craig Emory seemed to be at its end, that the Spirit confirmed my choice.

Like balmy waters pouring through me from the top of my head to the core of my being, suffusing every part of me with warmth and light, the Spirit spoke, testifying of my Heavenly Father's love for me and confirming that Craig Emory would indeed be a wonderful eternal companion for me. With it came bracing calm. I was shocked at how peaceful my voice sounded as I said, "All right, Craig. If that's what you think is best."

"What?" He turned toward me, swerving slightly before he regained control, and looking almost as shocked as he had in the store.

"I said that's all right with me, if you think it's best."

"You're not . . . upset?" I couldn't tell whether he was relieved or disappointed.

"Of course I'm upset," I heard myself saying, but my voice didn't sound the least bit unsettled. I gave myself a mental pat on the back. I paused, momentarily confronted by the words of sage mentors, most of them women I admired, all advising me not to tip my hand too soon, not to declare myself first, not to stop playing hard to get. But the Spirit's voice was even stronger, and I knew what I had to say.

"This isn't some game we're playing, Craig. It isn't just tomorrow or next year that we're talking about. It's all of eternity, and it isn't just my eternity or yours, either. It's the lives of generations yet unborn, people who might be our children or grandchildren or distant descendants—if we choose to be together. We both have to be certain it's right."

I laid my hand on his knee and tried to block out all the well-meaning advice I'd ever heard about letting the man lead. "I love you, Craig. I love you, very much."

He looked so uncomfortable. Here he was telling me he wanted to see other people, and I was declaring my love. It almost seemed unfair. If the Spirit hadn't been so strong, I might have taken pity on him and retracted my words.

Instead I paused, and I could feel my heart willing him toward me as I said, "I know how shaken you were by seeing Lisa again. It must have brought back all your doubts about your ability to make wise choices."

He didn't answer, but I saw him swallow hard, and I knew he was fighting back painful emotions.

"It's okay," I said, gently stroking his cheek and smoothing his curly hair around his ears. "Take all the time you need. If this is right, it will all work out."

He swallowed again. "You mean it?"

"Of course I mean it." The conviction in my voice was real. Then I lightened my tone. "Let's go on to Vernal and enjoy the weekend as we planned. After that, you do what you need to do. If you don't call me again for awhile, or if you choose to date other people, that will be your business. Then, when you've worked things out for yourself, if we belong together, we will be." I hugged his arm, my head on his shoulder, just to let him know where I wanted him to belong. Then I smiled as I added, "Just don't take too long. I can't wait forever."

He smiled back. He still didn't answer, but he took my hand from his knee and lifted my fingers to his lips. For a long moment he held them there, pressed against his kiss, and then he whispered, "Thank you." Again I felt the confirmation of the Spirit. However things turned out between us, it would be all right.

* * *

The tension eased between us after that. Craig was the celebrity guest and center of attention at the weekend's festivities, and he seemed to enjoy the praise lavished on him everywhere we went. That is, he seemed grateful for, though always a bit startled by, the attention. He introduced me simply as Sarah, ignoring speculative looks that searched for clues about our relationship, and I never volunteered any. I found that, surprisingly, I wasn't too worried what anyone else thought. When Great-Aunt Miriam asked if we were serious, I told her I hoped so, but I didn't feel the need to elaborate. I told myself things would work out the way they were supposed to, whether I pushed them or not.

Craig and I enjoyed the planned activities but also found time to be together outside the community's plans. We took a short drive into Flaming Gorge, hiked one short trail near the mouth of the canyon, and spent a quiet afternoon staring in awed wonder at the vanished denizens and startling petroglyphs in Dinosaur National Park. We kept the conversation light. We talked about the past (particularly the *way* past, when the dinosaurs were around), and we talked about the present—the gorgeous color in the gorge, the steep angle of the trails, the depth of the spring grasses, even the weather. What we carefully avoided was anything having to do with us or the future.

By Monday afternoon, things almost felt normal between us. That is, we had exhausted any remaining tension with hiking and driving and barbequing and careful avoidance of certain topics. I said a warm good-bye to Great-Aunt Miriam, who hugged me affectionately and said she'd love to have me come to visit someday when I could spend some time with her. Then I picked up the last of my things and waved good-bye as we started back toward home.

Craig maneuvered the pickup through the backstreets of Vernal and onto the main drag. We were merging into the open highway and picking up speed when he reached across and took my hand. "Thank you, Sarah."

"For what?"

"For this weekend. You've made it great."

"Hang on. You invited me. I should thank *you*, Craig. I've had a wonderful time."

"But I was so weird and moody . . . I wouldn't have blamed you if you had been pretty upset. Instead you made it a fun, great weekend full of happy memories."

Memories? Was he already thinking of me as part of his past? But then he kissed my fingers again. "Thank you."

"It's nothing," I answered, but it *was* something, and I was feeling that calm, peaceful assurance again as we headed down the road, our mood as breezy and comfortable as it had always been, especially when Craig rolled down the windows to let the warm spring breeze blow through.

We hadn't gone more than a few miles when we both noticed a small gray sedan far in the distance coming toward us on the opposite side of the highway, weaving out of its lane. The car swerved once, twice, and then the driver seemed to recover control. Craig said, "Wow, that was weird."

"I hope the guy isn't falling asleep."

"We'll just watch him until he gets past us." Craig was keeping a close eye on the oncoming vehicle while also glancing carefully around us, presumably making mental notes on possible escape routes.

There was a turn in the road then and a little dip, and we lost sight of the gray sedan. We didn't see it again until we turned into a road cut with steep-pitched embankments on either side. There was nowhere to go when the sedan suddenly jumped across the center line and came straight at us. Craig swerved to try to avoid the collision, and that was when everything shifted into super slow motion.

I'd often heard the cliché about how your life passes before your eyes. I didn't see any life scenes, but I did see everything that happened around us as if the events were a series of still pictures, and thoughts passed through my mind unhurriedly, as if I had endless time to think. I saw the sedan coming at us and realized that Craig had few options to get out of the way. I was sure the other driver would correct and safely pass us, then realized he had no time to correct.

I saw anxiety flash on Craig's face as his eyes went wide and his knuckles whitened, gripping hard on the wheel, and I heard the screeching noise as the tires on my side went up onto the road cut and skidded as Craig swerved to avoid the sedan that was now coming at us like a targeted missile. We came down hard off the side of the mountain just in time to meet the sedan's left front bumper with the left front of the truck, a glancing blow that sent us hurtling into a spin and then into the beginnings of a roll as our wheels hit loose sand just outside the road cut. I felt my seat belt sliding free and experienced a crystal moment of clarity when I realized it hadn't ever clicked when I fastened it. I felt the sickening lurch as the truck went over and had the clear realization that the accident was happening now, no matter what we did.

And then I was out the window and the truck was rolling away without me, and there was only one thought: *Father, please protect Craig! Please, please protect—* And then the screen went black.

Chapter 18

From somewhere far away, someone was calling my name. I wasn't sure how long I listened to it or how many times I heard it before it occurred to me that the sound meant something, that I was supposed to do something. I did know that I felt soothed by that familiar and wonderful voice, and that hearing it meant a great deal to me, although at the moment, I couldn't have told you why. Slowly, slowly the scene around me began to resolve into sharpened focus and I realized there were people around me—quite a number of them—and that they all seemed anxious and distressed. Then I saw the face that brought me back to myself and made me want to reenter the world. I whispered, "Craig?"

He shouldered a couple of burly fellows out of the way, stood closer to me, and took my hand. "Yes, Sarah. I'm here." He looked wonderful, whole, and healthy, his handsome features arranged in a look of concern and something a lot like love.

"You're okay?" I asked, my voice barely audible.

"I'm fine," he said, "perfectly fine. You're the one we're worried about."

"Don't worry," I answered, "I'm fine, too," but I think I said it only because that's what I was supposed to say. Honestly I couldn't have said for certain whether I was fine or not. Parts of me hadn't reported in yet, and it was hard to think around the swarms of bees and the heavy sandbags stuffing my brain.

"Get her some help—fast." Craig's voice was decisive, and the action around me seemed to shift into a higher gear—or maybe I just hadn't noticed before that I was on a gurney and being moved as we spoke.

I began to notice other things—the pale shirts and red suspenders of the volunteers from the Vernal Fire Department, the dark brown shirts and beehive shoulder patches of the state troopers, and the look of anxiety on everyone's faces. I wondered what was going on here . . . Then the moments before the accident flashed into sharp clarity. "The accident!" I said. "The sedan, the other car! What happened to—?"

"Shh, Sarah." Craig gripped my hand. "Don't worry about that now."

My voice was still squeaky, but I put more effort into it. "There was a man driving. I saw his face! Craig, is he—"

"Shh, love," Craig said again.

"Craig," I whispered, desperately needing to know.

He was silent for a moment, a pained look in his eyes. Then, finally, he gently said, "He didn't make it, Sarah."

"No. Oh, no." The first pain emerged through the fog, smacking me in a wide band across my forehead, stretching from ear to ear. "He crossed the middle," I said, grimacing, trying to lift my other hand to my head. It wouldn't move, and I realized it had been tied to the side of the gurney. I struggled to focus, to remember what I had just been saying. "He crossed the road. He came right at us. Why . . . ?"

"The paramedics think he had a heart attack, sweetheart." In the midst of everything else, the thought crossed my mind that he had never called me "sweetheart" before. It sounded odd, old-fashioned, but nice. "They think he may already have been gone before he hit us. That might even be why the accident happened."

"Oh." I paused, trying to understand. "Oh," I said again, beginning to feel the pain in my back and my left side, which started out dull but rapidly became so intense it was almost breathtaking. I gasped, uncertain whether I felt greater pity for the man who had lost his life today or for the agony in my own battered body. Tears were running down my face and pooling on my neck before I was even conscious of crying. "I hurt," I whimpered, sounding like a little kid with a boo-boo. "Please? I hurt."

"Can't you give her something for the pain?" Craig's question was a demand. "Help her!"

"We're doing what we can," a man's voice answered.

We reached the ambulance, and the gurney was folded down and rolled in. The bouncing and jostling caused such vivid, angry pain to shoot through me that I gasped as my moan turned into a near-scream. "Please!" I cried again. "Please? Something?"

"Help her!" Craig demanded again.

The same voice answered. "She's had a bad head injury. We won't be able to give her anything for the pain until we know how serious it is. We'll see what we can do for her after we get to the hospital."

"Hurry," Craig answered. "Please hurry."

There was some more jostling and then a prick in my arm that I barely felt, so heavy were the clouds of pain. Then the ambulance began to roll and the real pain began. "Craig!" I called. I couldn't turn my head, couldn't see him, and I feared we had left him behind.

"I'm here, Sarah." He took my hand again.

His presence calmed me. "Don't leave me." I gripped his fingers tightly.

"I won't," he promised.

A thought wandered at the edges of my mind. I struggled to get hold of it. "A blessing," I whispered. "I need a blessing."

Craig stroked my forehead. "We gave you one, Sarah. One of the paramedics is a high priest. He and I blessed you before you even woke up. You're going to be all right."

"Oh. Good." I thought about that for a moment. "Can I have another blessing? One I can hear?"

"I have oil," one of the attendants said. "We can bless her here if you like, or we can wait until we get to the hospital."

"I'll wait for the hospital," I decided. "Craig?"

"Yes, sweetheart?"

"Don't leave me. Please?"

"I won't," he said again. "I'm here, Sarah. I'm right here."

* * *

I got priority care at the Ashley Valley Medical Center. Apparently our accident was the most excitement they'd seen in days. Within a short few hours, I'd been poked, prodded, scanned, x-rayed, MRIed, and I'm not sure what else. Craig stayed right beside me through all of it—well, as much as they'd let him, except for the few minutes when the doctor insisted that he get checked out himself.

By nine o'clock, the staff emergency physician was ready to sit down with me—with us. She explained that my unplanned flight through the desert had ended in a sudden stop against a stone. I'd suffered a third-degree concussion, but she didn't see any sign of complications. I had also managed to wrap myself around a heavy creosote bush, which was why my back and left side hurt, but aside from a couple of bruised ribs and a small amount of internal bruising, I'd come through it all in pretty good shape.

"You'll need a couple of days of bed rest and observation to make sure there are no residual effects from your concussion," she concluded, "and you'll be sore for a few days, but other than that, it looks like you're going to be just fine. You're a very lucky young woman."

"Blessed," Craig corrected.

"Blessed," I repeated. "Doctor? Can I have something for the pain now?"

"I ordered it on my way in," she answered. A nurse entered the room with a couple of syringes on a tray. "It looks like it's here now. You have a restful evening, and I'll check on you in the morning."

The nurse explained what he was doing as he dripped the medication slowly into my IV. I felt it seconds later—a warm, stinging sensation as the medicine entered my vein, then a sudden easing of the war zone in my head and a fully relaxing, calming ease through the rest of my body as the pain was subdued by the chemicals.

"Oh, that feels good!" I moaned.

"Don't enjoy it too much. It's morphine," Craig said, but there was a teasing tone in his voice.

A short while later, Craig found another elder—it wasn't too difficult—and gave me the blessing he had promised. I was fuzzy enough from both the head-whack and the drug that I couldn't absorb everything that was said, but I distinctly heard him promise me quick healing and reduced pain. He also promised I would recover completely and go on to marry and bear children, and that I would have a long and healthy life full of service to family, community, and church. As he spoke, I again felt the peace that had come in the truck, the assurance that all would be well—with me, with us, with everything.

Before I slept I called my school district to let them know they'd need a sub for the rest of the week. Then I called Mr. Salazar's office voice mail and left the same message, with my apologies. That done, I felt brave enough to call my parents; I'd wanted to wait until I'd talked to the doctor before I called them. They were naturally shocked and distressed.

"We'll be there in four hours," Mom said, and I could hear her turning away from the phone to say, "We can leave immediately, can't we?" In the background my father's voice replied, "I'll throw some things in the car."

"No, Mom!" I said, pulling her back to our conversation. "That really won't be necessary. They're taking good care of me in the hospital here, and Craig hasn't left my side."

At that hint, Craig, who was standing right at my side, gestured that he'd like me to hand him the phone. "Mom? Craig wants to talk to you," I said, and handed it over.

"Sister Kimball?" Craig began. I heard only his half of the conversation, although it was fairly easy to guess what was happening on the other end. They repeated pretty much the same conversation I had already had with my mother, but when Craig told her about the two blessings he had given me, the intensity level in the room eased. He ended with, "Okay. Will do," and hung up the phone.

"Well?" I asked.

"She didn't promise that they aren't coming at all, but she said they won't try to come tonight. They're going to call in the morning."

"Good!" I breathed a deep sigh, glad my parents wouldn't be making a rush trip on that highway in the dark. "What was that last 'will do' about?"

"Your mom asked me to give you a hug for her," Craig answered. Then he leaned down and carefully took me into his arms. The hug was light and gentle, his every touch aware of my fragile and breakable condition. Yet I had never felt more secure, more cherished than I did at that moment. His touch also drained away the last of the anxiety I'd been feeling about my work and my parents. "I think I'm ready to sleep now," I said.

The nurse, making his late-evening rounds, suggested that perhaps Craig should leave now, maybe get a room in town. Craig insisted he wasn't going anywhere, and I heard the nurse ask, "Are you her husband?"

There was some mumbling between them then, but I thought I heard the word *fiancé*. I'd have to ask Craig about that—when I could keep my eyes open.

I woke once or twice during the night, and Craig was always right there, reclining in the lounge chair next to my bed. He brought me water, straightened my pillows, and got the nurse to bring painkillers when I woke up hurting. I couldn't have asked for a more kind or attentive caregiver. I didn't know what might pass between us once we left, but I had never felt more loved than Craig made me feel that night.

* * *

The two extra days in Vernal passed quickly. My parents called two or three times every day and seemed more reassured each time. Mom said my voice just kept getting stronger. Shari called more than once each day, and Jeanie called from Denver. My siblings all called, too—well, everyone but Mark, who would get the news about my accident the next weekend in his missionary e-mail from Mom. Great-Aunt Miriam came by to visit and brought both Craig and me some homemade apple pie.

Other than that, it was just the two of us during those two days, and I enjoyed Craig's company more than ever. We watched some old movies on TV and some DVDs from the nurses' station. Then, as my mind cleared, we played some board games and put together a rather challenging jigsaw puzzle picture of Bryce Canyon. I realized more and more how much Craig meant to me, how much I never wanted to be without him.

On Thursday morning, one week after I'd left home, I was released from the hospital. While I got my things together and dressed in the loose sweats Craig had bought for me locally, one of the hospital volunteers drove Craig to the shop where his truck had been towed. Remarkably, it had come through the accident with very minor damage, owing (the mechanic thought) to the odd "roll bar" in the back of the truck—the rack Craig used to carry his art, which he had so carefully and so recently checked and soldered. An hour later, Craig helped me back into the passenger seat, where he fastened the brand new seat belt himself, checking to be certain it was secure before he got in on the driver's side.

"Are you sure you're up to this?" Craig said as he started the engine.

I nodded. "I'm going to be fine. The doctors wouldn't have let me make the trip if they had any concerns."

"Just let me know if you think you need to stop or rest," he said.

After that, neither of us seemed to have much to say, and I wondered if he was as nervous as I was about starting this trip again. I felt a lump form in my throat and tears sting my eyes as we passed the road cut where everything had changed for us three days before. We could easily see the skid marks where Craig had tried to avoid the oncoming car. There were none from the sedan, and I remembered what the paramedics had said about that driver and how he had probably been gone before the accident even happened. I was glad that, if it was his time to leave, he hadn't had to go as a result of our accident.

I laid my hand on Craig's knee. "Thank you."

"For what?"

"For everything you've done for me these past few days—the blessings, the nursing care, everything—even bringing me on this trip. Thank you."

"Surely you can't be thanking me for what you've just been through. Sarah, I'm so sorry about all this—"

"Stop! Don't apologize," I said firmly. "You didn't do anything wrong. In fact, everything you've done has been wonderful. What happened here was just what the name implies, an accident—a sad, unfortunate accident. But you're okay, and I'm okay, and even the truck is okay. We have so much to be grateful for."

He nodded. "That's true. But you are good and generous to say so."

"Not generous. Blessed," I assured him. "And I have even more to be grateful for, because you've been so good to me. You know, my mom wouldn't have left me in the care of just anyone. She must know what a good guy you are." I smiled at him.

"If she'd known *this* was going to happen, she'd never have let you come."

I shook my head. "No one could have known this was going to happen, and the part before the accident was a great trip. I'm glad you asked me to come with you, Craig. It was a good idea." Then I paused, fortified my courage, and brought up the subject that had nagged at me all week. "Listen, about what you said before . . . When we get home, if you want to spend some time apart, maybe date other people for awhile . . ."

Craig veered the truck sharply to the right, and I gasped, fearing we might be having another accident, but he straightened the wheels and cruised to a stop on the shoulder. Then he turned off the engine, put on the parking brake, and loosened his seat belt, sliding closer to me. "That—what I said in the truck before? That was a bad idea, one of the worst I ever had. I said those things because I got scared—"

"Because you saw Lisa," I filled in for him. "Because you remembered how things went before, and you were afraid of going there again."

"Because I was afraid," he said pointedly. "That was before I knew what *real* fear was." He took my hand. "Sarah, I'd never been as scared in all my life as I was when I saw you go out that truck window. Then, when I finally got out of the truck and I couldn't find you . . ." He swallowed hard, and there were tears in his eyes.

"Sarah, you deserve better than this. You deserve a splendid ring and the down-on-one-knee bit, and the whole romantic scene, and I promise I'll follow through with all that just as soon as I get the chance, but I can't let you out of my sight until I know that I'll never lose you again."

He lifted my fingers to his lips and kissed them sweetly, just as he had a week earlier, when we had first come this way. Then he held both my hands, and his voice trembled as he asked, "Sarah Kimball, will you marry me?"

An odd thought came into my head at that moment—an image of how really awful I must look in my ill-fitting sweats and loose, still-damp hair, without makeup and with tears running down my cheeks. If Craig loved me now, if he had loved me through the ugly hours in the hospital, then surely he could love me forever.

I grinned through my tears. "I love you, Craig Emory. Of course I'll marry you."

He pulled me against him and kissed me soundly. Cars flew by us on the highway, but it was some time before we were on our way again, starting out once more on the road to forever.

Epilogue

Noah and Shari were married this morning in the Jordan River Temple, and Kerry will soon be sealed to them. It was a beautiful ceremony, but then, it was the first sealing I've ever seen. I imagine they must all be beautiful—simple, elegant, graced by the Spirit. I went through the Bountiful Temple with them and other family members yesterday, and that too was beautiful—and timely, since Craig and I are planning a wedding of our own next month.

He followed through with the ring and the romantic proposal, just as he promised he would. I've decided to keep the details for us alone, but suffice it to say that I am wearing a beautiful diamond ring, designed just for me by a skilled artist who may soon be starting a new career as a jewelry designer as well—given the way the jeweler oohed and aahed over Craig's sketches.

Things have gone well for our plans so far. We are grateful that Craig's paperwork came through quickly and that we aren't having to wait like Noah and Shari did. As soon as our engagement was official, we called the mission office in Belgium and got permission to call Craig's parents. That's how I "met" my future in-laws—over the phone. They seem like perfectly lovely people. They were very kind to me and obviously happy for Craig. His mother just kept telling him, "You deserve some happiness, dear. You deserve happiness." They are completing their mission in about three weeks, which is why our wedding is in four. We promised we'd wait until after they got home. We called Craig's brothers, too. Ryan and his wife will fly out for the wedding. Phil agreed he "might" come to the reception.

We also got permission to call Mark. He put Craig through some difficult, only-a-brother-would-ask-that questions, just as Noah, Seth, Josh, and Tim had done, and then he asked us to wait to be married until after he got home. But Mark's release date isn't until October. We promised him we would take lots of pictures.

Speaking of pictures, I've been at the chapel all morning, taking digital shots of the minimalist Asian design Craig created for Shari and Noah's reception. It's so beautiful, I want to make sure I know how to reproduce parts of it when we have our own reception next month, though I'll probably go for paler colors, with lots of white and ivory and maybe some orchids.

Shari has decided to teach next year. Noah hesitated at first; he was eager to start their family, but he agreed that they could wait a few months while Shari got a little teaching experience and while the three of them—he and Shari and Kerry—all learn how to be a family. Then they will begin the process of enlarging their family portrait and giving Kerry a sibling. Eventually they hope for five or six, a big family these days—even in Utah.

Craig and I are thinking four, but we'll take our family as it comes. We've decided that's one of the best things about being a couple—enjoying the adventure together, taking it as it comes. Craig saw how happy I was to get back to my little brood of third graders before the school year ended, and he agreed I should teach another year before we start our family. Like Noah, he was eager to start our family right away—he will turn thirty in August, and he says he can hear his clock ticking—but he knows we will both have some adjustments to make, since every couple does, and he agreed it might be best if we spent some time as a couple before we start filling up all the extra bedrooms in his house.

Craig has been "readying" his house for me. I told him it doesn't need any changes, but he is putting new pots and pans in the kitchen, clearing out drawers in the master bath, and emptying the storage out of a large walk-in closet off the bedroom. Knowing I'd soon be missing Harry, he took me to the animal shelter, where we adopted a little tabby kitten, so he's put a cat door between the house and the garage. He named the kitten Renoir, but we call him Rennie. Ruth will pet-sit at the house for us while we're on our honeymoon—a trip for which Craig is carefully guarding his secret plans.

Since I'll be moving into Craig's home next month, I put my own house on the market. Real estate has been slow lately, but I got a reasonable offer within the first two weeks, and it should close the week before the wedding.

Something I didn't know until after we were officially engaged—I guess Craig didn't want to brag—is that my fiancé is more than just "comfortable," financially speaking. His art has been so successful that he has already paid off his home and the renovations on it. He owns his truck and his furniture, has no debts, and has started some solid savings and investment accounts—not to mention having a healthy year's supply in his basement. Not only am I getting the kindest, most attractive, most amazing man I've ever met, I'm also getting the benefit of his exceptional artistic skill and good financial planning. If we are sensible, we will never have to worry about money.

I couldn't help teasing him about all this, considering his earlier warning. "I thought you said you weren't good with money," I said as we left his accountant's office.

He grinned. "I never said that. What I *said* is I can't balance a checkbook. That's why I hired an accountant."

Craig recommended I take all the proceeds from the sale of my home and put them into a retirement account in my own name. I'm planning to follow through with that—with one exception. After some serious thought and prayer, I e-mailed Sam and got him to send me the mailing address for Kyle and Beth Lewis. When the house sells, they will get a check equal to Kyle's share of the original down payment, plus a few percentage points in interest. I told Craig about it, and he liked the idea. This is the final step I need to take to put the past behind me. With good timing, the check should help them buy their own family home. It feels like the right thing to do. In a way, I owe them.

When Craig suggested I write down the story of our meeting and courtship, I knew I couldn't start with the day we met. I learned so much during that year between Kyle and Craig—so much about love and faith, so much about the Atonement, so much about acceptance and leaving judgment to the Lord. Kyle and Beth Lewis played important roles in that process. Though the lessons were painful, I'm thankful for them. I may never see or hear of the Lewises again, but I want their last thought of me to be positive.

Happy and positive—that's the way Craig and I are beginning our life together. Just last night he told me he has never seen me happier. I answered, "You've just never seen me so much in love." In fact, my life is filled with love. I love my Savior. I love His gospel and His Church. I love my family and my work. I love Craig more than I could have imagined possible, and I know I'll only love him more tomorrow. As I look back on our accident near Vernal, I know it was just another step in the careful path along which a loving Heavenly Father has led us both, bringing us to this wonderful, lovely place in our lives.

As we look to the future, we know things will not always be happy. Like all couples, Craig and I will have to face our own bumps in the road, but we have learned to trust the Savior. We know that wherever He leads us will be exactly where we need to go. And we are looking forward to the journey.

About the Author

Susan Aylworth started her first "novel" at the age of nine and declared her ambition as a writer at a fifth-grade Career Day. Now a novelist and playwright with deep roots in the west, she was born in Mesa and raised in northeastern Arizona near the Four Corners. Susan eventually attended college in Utah, where she met and married journalist Roger Aylworth. She has raised her family of seven children in northern California, where she teaches writing and literature at a state university. Previous works include a series of novels set in fictional Rainbow Rock, Arizona, a play about Hamlet's mother, and fifteen grandchildren.